Just One OF THE boys

Just One OF THE boys

LEAH AND KATE ROOPER

Entangled Publishing, LLC
2614 South Timberline Road
Suite 109
Fort Collins, CO 80525
Visit our website at www.entangledpublishing.com.

Crush is an imprint of Entangled Publishing, LLC.

Edited by Brenda Chin
Cover design by Cover Couture
Cover art from Shutterstock

Manufactured in the United States of America

First Edition October 2017

To Pat and Johnny
Go Hawks!

Chapter One

ALICE

I'm not sure why everyone in the movies gets so down about moving. In my opinion, moving is pretty darn awesome. New house, bigger room—finally out of suburbia and into the big city! Most kids would be devastated to go through twelfth grade in a new school, but I prefer to look on the bright side. I already have a bucket list of things I want to do in Chicago before school starts...and I'm not talking about deep-dish pizza or Wrigley Field.

It's what I'm doing right now.

I take a deep breath as I lace up my skates. The sound of the lace slipping through the grommets is reassuring. All the mottos and mantras every coach has drilled into my mind repeat in my head. Believe in yourself. Visualize yourself as a winner.

Because this isn't any ordinary practice. It isn't even a game.

This is the tryouts for the Chicago Falcons.

I grin over at my twin brother, Alexander. He shakes his head and runs a hand through his straggly brown hair.

"Don't be nervous," I say.

"Easy for you to say, Al," he mumbles.

I strap on my helmet. When we're like this, we're pretty much identical. Same height, same smile. Our old teammates back home used to get us confused all the time.

I throw on one of the plain white jerseys they've given us. The black number is my only identification out there. I tuck my long hair into my helmet and go through my breathing again. Skates are laced, pads are tied, and my helmet is on. Only thing to do is head out onto the rink.

When my blades hit the ice, it's like I can breathe, as if I've been drowning and finally coming up for air.

It's all in the crisp smell of the rink, the cold air flowing over my face as I do a few laps. This may be a new arena in a new city, but once I'm on the ice, it's all the same. My stick is like an extension of my hands. My skates feel like a part of me.

As I do a few laps around the ice, I picture it in my mind's eye: playing for the Chicago Falcons. Not only are they one of the biggest junior league hockey teams in all of North America, their players are also a favorite of NHL scouts.

A jab of longing rings in my chest, but I push it back. Okay, whatever, I know an NHL scout will never look at me — due to having the wrong parts and all — but that doesn't mean I can't play here. This league is still highly competitive and the players...well, they're good.

And I know I'm good enough to join them.

The Chicago Falcons may never have had a girl on the team before, but technically the league doesn't have any rules against it. I know I can out-skate and outplay any boy in these tryouts. All I have to do is show the coach what I'm made of.

Someone bumps me from behind. I don't even have to

look...twin sixth sense, and all that. I give Xander a smile he doesn't return.

I can see it in the way he's skating. His knees lock, and his strides are jagged.

"Hey, just play your game," I say.

We take a couple practice shots at the net, but he misses every time. "Everyone here is so *big*," he says.

I look around. At 5'9, we'd be considered tall in a normal setting. But in the hockey world...well, we could use a couple more inches.

"No one's as fast as us."

"No one's as fast as *you*," he says.

"Yeah, well," I bump him on the shoulder, "you're always right behind me."

"What if I don't fmake it..." he mutters softly. "Then all these years...it's all been for nothing. Just don't show me up out there."

I roll my eyes. Xander can be so melodramatic sometimes. But I'm used to it. We've been playing hockey together our whole lives. I know Ma would prefer if I stuck to figure skating, but there's just something about the stick, the puck, and the pure rush of adrenaline when hitting the net that I can't resist. And Xander — well, he tags along for everything I do.

Xander was always stronger than me, so I had to adapt. Learning to outskate and outplay the boys was the only way to keep my blades on the ice. I topped my last league in points and shoot-out goals.

The coach skates out to the middle of the rink; he's big, with a half bald head and one of those moustaches that looks like it belongs on the bottom of a Zamboni. White-haired and wrinkled, but built like an ox. I gulp.

He doesn't have to introduce himself for me to know who he is. Coach Zabinski. I wonder if any of the other players here did a full history check on him like I did. I could ace a test on "Zabinski Stats from 1978". As an ex-NHL player, you would expect him to have one of the best teams in the league, but the Falcons haven't made the playoffs in years.

I'm about to change that.

Right now, he's lecturing the group on what it takes to be a Falcon, but I don't need to hear it. I know it. I know I have what it takes.

Then—the drills begin! Skating, shooting, defense. Scrimmage after scrimmage.

My heart pounds, working overtime in my chest, and my muscles tense with each length of the rink. I know I need to concentrate on my game, but I can't help eyeing up the competition.

Here I was thinking I was going to play with the best of the best. Instead, I'm surrounded by glorified goons. I should know all about that, figuring my own boyfriend is one of those goons now playing in Detroit. But that's not what the Falcons need. They need a playmaker, a speedster, an all-star.

THWACK! My favorite sound. My puck hits the net during shooting trials.

BRIING! I cringe as Xander's puck sails off the post.

"Goddammit," he swears as he skates up beside me. "You're killing me here, Al."

I nudge him in the ribs. "Maybe I'll make you my roadie."

Finally, the whistle goes, and we surround Coach Zabinski.

I take a deep breath, quieting the nervous energy within me. I concentrate on the crisp, familiar smell of the rink. The warmth of my body beneath my pads and jersey. The feeling of my feet, attached to my skates, grounded to the ice. It's like a lifeline.

Around me, the others shuffle and pant. A few shoot dirty looks my way. *Should have skated faster, then maybe*

I wouldn't have stolen the puck from you. Xander's face is flushed, his eyes downcast. He knows it. He didn't perform to a Falcons' level.

I stare at Coach's mouth, nearly hidden behind his Zamboni moustache. Say it. Say the names of those who made it.

I tighten my mitt around the stick. This is my moment.

"All right," Coach says, his voice a raspy grunt. "You played hard out there. Some harder than others. There has to be more than potential to make the Falcons. You have to have skill. Passion. And you have to skate hard." I swear he looks at me through his forested eyebrows. "Only four of you made the team. The rest — well, try again next year. Or don't, and save me the trouble of cutting you twice. Ready? Okay."

My heart threatens to rip right through my jersey. But he looked at me. I skated hard.

"Number fifty-two. Howard. Congratulations." A whoop goes up from a thick dude with mutton chops. "Number twenty-five. O'Donnell. Congratulations. Number eighty-nine. Stickly. Congratulations."

My lip tremors. Only one spot left. There's a part of me that feels like I should reach out and take Xander's hand… but not here. Not now.

"Number seventeen. Bell. Congratulations."

A flood of relief and adrenaline floods through me. A smile threatens to break my face.

"You did it!" Xander says, forcing me into a huge hug. He's got a matching grin, but I know his face better than mine. His eyes are downturned, his mouth too wide.

"I'm sorry, buddy," I say. I know I should control myself, but I can't. "I did it! I'm on the Falcons! I'm a Falcon!"

I jump up and down, pounding my skates into the ice until shaves of frost fly away like wings. The other chosen ones have gathered around Coach Zabinski as the losers skate off to dwell in their suckiness.

Hah.

I'm a winner. A Falcon. And all those boys wish they could have skated like me!

My face is sticky with sweat and hurts from smiling. The first girl to ever make the Falcons! I skate over and throw my helmet off, shaking out my long hair. The air is so cool on my face and—

Coach stares at me as if I'd just told him football was the most interesting sport in the world. His left eye twitches.

And he's not the only one. The other chosen ones— Mutton Chops, O'Poodle, whatever their names were—are giving me that same gawking look.

"What?" I finally snap.

Coach clears his throat. He looks down at his clipboard and then back up at me, then down at his clipboard. "N-number seventeen? Al Bell?"

"Yeah," I say. "Short for Alice."

"Alice. Well, wouldn't that have been nice to know." He clears his throat again and pulls his clipboard to his chest. "I'm afraid I made a mistake. I meant to say the other Bell. Number forty-four."

Xander, about to step off the ice, turns. "Me?"

"Yes!" Coach calls. "Come here, son!"

"What are you talking about?" I say, my voice raising an octave. "You called MY name! You said number seventeen! That's me!"

"Dude," Howard scoffs, "you're a chick."

A growl rises up my throat. "And I outshot you three to one. I don't know why the hell Coach wants you on the team, figuring how bad your stick handling was but—"

"You want me?" Xander skates up right beside Coach. "Me? On the Falcons?"

"I said Bell, didn't I?" Coach grumbles. "Well, you're on

the team."

"It's not fair! I skated circles around everyone here!" I push myself right up under that damned Zamboni. "Coach, give me a chance."

Coach turns and skates toward the boards. "New players, follow me." He turns his head back and glares. "And that doesn't mean you, missy."

He storms off the ice and everyone follows him. Xander gives a sympathetic shrug as he skates away. I'm alone on the ice.

Okay, correction. Chicago totally blows.

• • •

HAYDEN

I pull my Jeep into the parking lot of the arena. The late afternoon sun casts an orange glow across the pavement. The wind blows in my face.

The wind always blows in my face here.

Coach Zabinski said the ice would be free after tryouts today, so the boys and I figured it would be nice to come and mess around on the rink before practice starts up again for the season. We meet up in the parking lot, duffel bags hoisted on our shoulders, and head toward the arena.

There's a bunch of kids leaving; you can tell who's been cut just by the looks on their faces.

"New recruits," Tyler Evans says, waving at a couple kids as we head in. His niceness is obnoxious most of the time, but today it just slides off me. Today will be a good day. No drills, no scouts, just good ol' fashion hockey.

We head past Coach on the way in. I was thinking about trying to feel him out and see if he's still pissed at me for the end of last season, but he's getting an earful from some scraggily boy who obviously didn't make the team.

"Someone's bitter," Daniel Sacachelli laughs, clapping me on the back. "I guess we can't all be Hayden Tremblay."

I know I never fought to get into this league the way these rookies did: I was offered a spot a year ago, when my brother Kevin and I moved here from Winnipeg, Manitoba. I was only sixteen, but I scored more points than anyone else that season.

Yeah, some of the older guys were mad when I started, but they shut up when I hit the ice.

Or when they saw the name on the back of my jersey.

Most of the rookies leaving give us a wide berth. They all look so little. Was I this stupid and starstruck when I arrived? I can't remember.

One of them stops in front of me. "Hayden Tremblay?" he stutters. I try to get around him, but he starts walking backward, his eyes gaping at me. I just want to hit the ice.

"Yeah," I finally say.

"Oh my god." He smiles. He's got a patchy excuse for a beard. "I'm Ned. I just made the team. It's so cool to meet you!"

"Yeah." I deke around him.

"Your brother..."

And here it comes.

"...is so freaking awesome. When he got named the youngest captain in the NHL—"

"Amazing," I mutter and walk off. Damn it, I don't even look like Kevin. How did that newbie know it was me? While Kevin resembles a well-kept blond lumberjack, I got the dark eyes and hair from Mom's side of the family. At least I somehow managed to get an extra inch of height on my older brother. It doesn't matter that I scored the most points in the junior league last season (despite being suspended five games) when my brother is the captain of Chicago's NHL team.

I'll never live up to that.

I throw my bag on the bench, lace up my skates, and head onto the ice. Sometimes I hate how good it feels to be out here. I wish I could just say screw it and walk away from it all...but I can't. I need this as much as I need to breathe.

A few laps around the rink and we're ready to play.

"Heads up!" I deke around the net.

"Not again!" Evans groans, reaching with his stick in a last desperate attempt to foil me.

Hah. I slam the puck against the back of the net.

"Get a new move, Tremblay," Sacachelli says in his thick Long Island accent. Black, oily strands of hair creep out from under his helmet. I wonder why he uses so much hair product when he's just going to sweat it out on the ice.

I flash a grin. "I will—when you figure out how to beat that one."

I skate backward, giving them a victorious fist pump. Sometimes I wonder why Ev and Sacs still play with me all the time. I can't think of a single time in the last year when they've won.

"All right, hotshot," Evans says, showing off some fancy stickhandling. "Let's see your defense."

Tyler Evans, Daniel Sacachelli, and I have been playing for the Chicago Falcons for a year now. And with the new season just around the corner, it's hard not to think about it. Because that's what playing for the Falcons does. It consumes you. Practice. Game. Eat food, drink water, work out, pose for photos, go to charity events, sleep. "Enjoy" mandated relaxation time...everything is all governed by Coach Z. Relaxation time is not relaxing when it's forced into your schedule.

But right now, I don't have to worry about hitting the net in order to maintain my rep as top scorer. I just have to score to take Sacs' ego down a few notches.

Back and forth, we burst up and down the rink. A quick

deke, a spin, and my puck connects with the net for the third time since we started.

We take a break and Evans pants hard, hunched over with his stick across his knees. He's smaller than Sacs and I, and somehow managed to make it this far without a single broken nose or lost tooth. "Slow down and let the rest of us have a chance, eh, Tremblay?"

I laugh and slap him on the back. Right now I don't think I could slow down if I tried.

Sacachelli skates over to me and flicks his eyes to the stands. "Looks like we've got a celebrity in the audience."

My blood goes cold before I even look up.

Why the hell is he here?

I turn and stare into his eyes. Kevin Tremblay. Number Two. Captain of the hottest NHL team in the league. Winner of the Calder Trophy. Current record holder for most points in a rookie season. And my older brother.

My grip tightens on my stick and I turn away. Evans has noticed him and looks up like he's some damn godly idol. "Are we playing?" I snap.

We get back into the game but I feel Kevin's eyes on me like a laser. *What is he doing here?* I lose the faceoff. When I finally muscle the puck back, I take a shot but miss the goal by at least a meter. His voice rings in my head: *"You know that move, Hayden. We've practiced it. Keep your stick on the ice."*

Heat rises to my face. I can feel his eyes watching my every movement: how I glide, how I hold the stick, how my head is raised. He steeples his fingers beneath his chin, watching, deciding, judging—

"Don't mind if I do!" Sacachelli flashes me his slimy grin and easily lifts the puck off my stick. "Smell ya later!" He snickers and turns, taking the puck with him.

I look down at my empty stick, then back up at my brother

in the bleachers. Stupid Kevin. His voice rings in my head again: *"Rookie mistake, Hayden. Think you're going to make it to the NHL when you lose a puck that easily?"* If he hadn't come here, I wouldn't have lost the puck!

I roar, and my muscles spasm beneath me as I force myself down the ice with a ferocity I haven't had all summer. Sacs is lolly-gagging ahead, still laughing, getting ready to pass to Evans, who has a clean shot at the net.

Screw that.

I throw my whole body against Sacachelli. He sails across the ice like a rag doll.

I don't care. This is hockey. The puck is right in front of me. I pull my stick back and smash it against the puck.

The puck sails across the ice, missing the net by a foot.

"ARGH!" I scream, throwing my stick to the ground and whipping off my helmet.

Evans drops his stick and rushes over to Sacs. "Dude!"

I throw one glance toward Sacs, whose clutching a bloody nose, but looks otherwise fine. Evans is holding a glove to his spurting snoz.

Shit.

I've done it again.

All of Coach and Kevin's words from last season come roaring down on me. Every single one of their disappointed lectures.

I storm off the ice and into the locker room. I throw everything into my duffel bag in a quick huff. I want to get out of here before I have to talk to anyone. Especially Kevin.

But of course, I can't get that lucky. As soon as I step out into the parking lot, I see him leaning against my Jeep.

Kevin was always faster than me.

"I don't feel like talking," I yell from across the parking lot.

"That's perfect," he calls back, "because I do."

My whole body tenses up and I avoid eye contact as I approach him. Kevin's gaze is so intense that once he gets you in his tractor beam, you can't escape.

I stand beside him and fumble with my keys. Kevin may be older than me, but he's slightly shorter, even a little smaller. It doesn't matter. Standing next to him, I always feel three feet tall.

"What are you doing here?" I grumble.

"I'm worried about you," he says. His voice is low, a purring rumble like a car engine or a coffee machine. "I haven't seen you around our house."

"You mean your house?" I say.

"You know Eleanor and I always want to see you upstairs." He scratches his thick blond beard.

"Okay. Thanks." Living in my brother's basement suite was supposed to give me independence. I don't need him and his fiancée babying me. I stopped being a kid over a year ago, when Mom and Dad…

I shake my head. I'm not going to give Kevin the satisfaction of a real heart-to-heart.

Kevin walks around to the other side of the Jeep and gets in.

I throw my bag in the back and slam the door. "Where's your car?"

"Eleanor dropped me off." Of course, he planned this whole thing.

I start the Jeep. It creaks and groans and rattles and makes every other sort of noise that reminds you of an old man on a deathbed. It's a bona fide piece of shit, but I paid for it myself, and I'll be damned if I let Kevin own another part of me. I may have to rely on him for food, and a place to live, but the less he feels like he's the savior of my world, the better.

"What do you say we grab dinner tonight? Catch up. Talk

about the new season. Falcons got a lot to prove coming up."

Bubbles of indignation rush through me. "Aren't you sick of talking about hockey? It's press release after press release."

"Come on," he says, flashing me that smile the newspapers love. The one they put on the cover of *Hockey News* that read TREMBLAY NAMED YOUNGEST CAPTAIN IN NHL HISTORY. "You know we never get sick of talking about hockey."

My grip tightens on the wheel. "Speak for yourself."

"Hayden," Kevin says, and puts a hand on my shoulder. "Talk to me. We've hardly spoken about the upcoming season at all." I shoot a look back at him. His mouth is downturned, brown eyes narrowed. He looks more like Dad every day.

I hate it.

"What is there to talk about?" I snap back.

"Zabinski's going to pick a new captain," Kevin says. "Let me help you. We could train together. There's going to be NHL scouts all over the place this season. I really think you have what it takes—"

My knuckles lose color and the speedometer shoots up another five miles. "I *know* I have what it takes. What, you think because you're some big shot in the NHL now that I can't do it here? I led the Falcons in goals last year—"

"Hayden," he says, "the Falcons didn't make the playoffs."

"That's not my fault. I wasn't playing the last few games."

"Exactly," he says softly. "You were suspended. You weren't there to lead your team when they needed you. You've got to rein it in. You've got to focus."

I turn onto Ridge Boulevard and try to concentrate on the road. "You've said all this before."

"Then listen." His stringy blond hair falls in his face. "And don't—"

"Don't do this. Do that instead. I get it, okay?"

"Don't interrupt me." I can feel his glare burrowing through the side of my head. I'm getting on his nerves. I feel like I might be the only one who can. Eternally calm, focused, unemotional Kevin. Captain Stoic. "If you focus this season, you could break records and win—"

"I broke records last season," I mutter.

"Breaking the record for the most fights in a season isn't one you should be proud of."

"And what records should I be breaking, oh glorious *capitaine*?" We turn off the freeway and onto a road filled with row after row of beautiful high-end condos and houses. "Every record you've already broken?"

I pull into the driveway. The stone house with the perfectly coiffed lawn and steeped roof looms before me as my own personal prison. I yank the keys out of the ignition and let them fall on my lap. Kevin runs his hands over his face and rests his head against the back of the seat.

"Look," he says, "you know if you didn't want to play in the NHL, I would just leave you alone, right?"

"You'd never leave me alone," I mutter.

"What I mean is, Hayden, I don't care if you play in the NHL. Mom and Dad…they never cared, either. But you're my little brother. I know you. And I know this is your dream. And to watch you just throw it away…"

"How am I throwing it away?" I spit. "I played every game I could last season. I came to every practice."

"I just want to see you try again," Kevin says, his hands restless on his lap. "This last year, you've just been floating by, and you can get away with it because your 60% is as good as everyone else's 100%."

Kevin's favorite thing in the world is percentages. I'm pretty sure he stays up at night just thinking of ways he can add percentages into everyday conversation.

"But I know what you can do at 100%. Heck, I've seen you give 200%! And it's like you've just given up. Maybe you're angry with me or angry with the world for what it's done to us. But don't you see? You're only hurting yourself."

"I'm 100% done with this conversation," I say and open the door to the Jeep.

Of course, Kevin can't just let me go. "Where's the kid who got up with me at five a.m. every morning to go running? Where's the guy who stayed at the rink until the Zamboni driver kicked us out? Where's the boy who did laps around the track wearing weights just to build muscle? Where's my little brother?"

I don't even look at Kevin. I get out and slam the door. "Well, maybe he died, too."

Chapter Two

I can't even fathom how wrong I was last week. Chicago is *not* amazing. It's not okay. It's just a windy slab of concrete where dreams go to die. I never thought I'd miss our little boring town, but after two weeks in Chicago, I'd happily move to Mars.

I follow the monotone directions of the GPS on my dashboard. I don't know why I agreed to pick Xander up. He's been so chipper the last few days; I want to tell him to turn his thousand-watt personality down a few notches. Usually I'm the optimist, the cheerer-upper of his sour moods. But now Xander's on the Chicago Falcons, and he's joined this weird theater club. If he loves everything about Chicago so much, he should also love its transit system.

"You have arrived," the GPS says. Luckily there are hardly any other cars around — an anomaly in this godforsaken city — and I park in front of a door with peeling red paint. A sign hangs above it - The Red Butterfly Theater Club.

I know if I just wait in the car, it'll be eons before Xander shows his face. So I yank the door open and walk in.

All around me, theater kids buzz around, like little workers bees in their hive. I can't understand why Xander wants to be a part of this. I told him he should give up his weird theater hobby once he made the Falcons. Instead, he should be spending every free moment at the rink, practicing. But I have to be supportive. I've gone to every one of his plays all the way from Baby Jesus to Romeo, because God knows Mom won't.

But I'm in absolutely no mood to be around theater kids today. Their peppy cheerfulness is already getting on my nerves.

A tall dude with a stack of scripts does a double take as he walks passed me. "Xan—?"

I roll my eyes and pull my long hair out from my hoodie. I'm long over being offended when someone mistakes me for my brother. "I'm his sister."

The bearded guy narrows his eyes. "Trippy."

I sigh. "Do you know where I can find him?"

"Through there, in the theater." He points toward a set of big black doors but doesn't take his eyes off me. "It's so weird. Who knew Xander could be hot?"

"Disgusting." I storm off through the doors. Boy, does Xander ever owe me for making me deal with these people.

I walk into a large, empty auditorium. I trail my fingers along the run-down black seats as I head toward the stage. My footsteps echo through the room.

"Hey, Al."

I look up to see Xander balanced on the top of a ladder, hanging felt stars to the curtains.

"Are you ready?"

"Just one more minute," he calls down.

I flop into one of the seats. One more minute for Xander

in the theater means another two hours.

"So how were the tryouts?" he calls down. His voice echoes mockingly through the theater: "*outs...outs...outs.*"

I slide even further into the chair, wishing it would swallow me whole. "I didn't make it." I've been so down about the Falcons, Xander found a local women's recreational hockey team for me to try out for.

"What?" Xander says, twisting around to look at me. The ladder shudders precariously with his movement. "How did you not make it? They let, like, sixty-year-olds on that team."

"It's not that I wasn't good enough," I mutter. "They told me I wasn't a good fit for the team."

"How were *you* not a good fit?" Xander says. He turns back to his felt stars. There's still a huge stack on one of the rungs below him.

"I may have accidentally given the captain a bloody nose."

"Accidentally?"

"She went face first into the boards—"

I can see Xander's eyebrow rise even from down here.

"—after I checked her." I bury my face into my hands. "I needed the puck!"

"You know," Xander says, "women's hockey is traditionally non-contact." He's half-hanging off the ladder as he stretches to place a star.

"I've never played women's hockey, though!" Our little town only had one hockey league, and they didn't care that I was a girl, even though I was the only one. Xander and I have played on the same team since we started skating.

I guess I always knew if I wanted to play professional hockey, I'd have to join an all-girls team eventually...but it never mattered to me what level I played at, as long as I could play, as long as I had a team, as long as I was challenged (but still the best.)

I go over it for the millionth time in my head. I *was* the best at that tryout. Xander was mediocre at best. I know the coach meant me. He just didn't want a girl on the team.

My hands twist into fists in my lap. It's not *fair*. There's no rule against girls in the league! Coach Zabinski is just a sexist loser who was threatened a girl could outplay all those boys.

Xander sighs, and it reverberates throughout the auditorium, as if there's four other disappointed brothers voicing their disapproval with me.

"You've got to *try* to be happy, Alice," he says. He climbs a rung higher on the ladder, and stretches upwards to place the decorations. "Things are going good. Can't you be happy for me?"

"Of course I'm happy for you. But—"

"Stop!" he yells, and the ladder shakes beneath him. "No more buts! Stop thinking about yourself for once. NHL scouts love drafting from the Falcons. If I play a good season..."

Xander hasn't played a good season in his life.

"Don't roll your eyes. Just listen." Xander runs his hands through his dark hair. "I could really make something of myself. If I play well, no one would look down on me ever again. This could be a fresh start for both of us."

Xander has always talked about making it big. I never really thought about it, for obvious reasons. But I guess he's right. Maybe with the right training and coaching from the Falcons, he could make it.

"Just have a good cry and get over it," Xander says.

"Hah!" The laugh chokes out of my throat. "You know I don't cry." Even though I haven't been this mad and hurt since...well, since Dad left. I haven't passed a tear since. I don't think I know how to anymore. "And I don't get over things. I get revenge!"

Xander ignores me. "Then think of the good stuff. You can still play hockey. You can help me practice."

"I will be at the rink a lot," I mutter.

"What do you mean?"

I pull my hood over my face, too ashamed to look at him. "Mom called me…"

"Uh oh…"

"And I was feeling super depressed about not making the women's team."

"Yeah…"

"So I maybe sorta agreed to be part of her two charity figure skating events."

He looks at me for a moment then bursts out laughing, "But you hate figure skating!"

"I *knowww*!" I say and slide off the chair and onto the floor. "But I need to be skating somehow or I'll die. And she was guilt tripping me. It's apparently a huge deal in this city! What was I supposed to say?"

"At least Mom will finally shut up about how no one ever helps her with her charity functions," Xander says, picking up the last few felt stars. "So what? Are you going to be running around in one of those silly tutus every night?"

"There's just one silly promotional event," I say. "And then the big charity dance in the spring. The Ice Ball, or something stupid like that. I'll be performing a solo."

Xander throws his head back and laughs. "You know you can't hit things in figure skating, right? You'll be too busy performing your double axels, and toe loops, and pirouettes."

"A pirouette is ballet, idiot." I laugh anyway.

Xander throws his hands over his head and points his toes on the rungs. "Elvis Stojko, eat your heart out!"

"Be careful!" I say, but a smile breaks out on my face.

"And what about this one? A catch-foot, right?" Xander reaches behind his head, groping for his foot. He balances on the rung with only one leg.

I clutch my stomach and let my laugher chase away the

terrible day. Maybe Xander's right. Maybe this is a good thing for us. This could be a big break for the whole family.

With a huge, careless grin on his face, Xander shifts his weight, and the ladder lurches beneath him. Within a split second, his smile turns to terror, as he falls through the air, and lands on the stage with a triumphant *crack*.

. . .

The bright light of the hospital pounds against my eyelids. I sit in a chair beside Xander's hospital bed. He sprawls across the stark white sheets so pathetically, I'm reminded of road kill. They stuck us in a shared room in the pediatric ward, and faded stickers of Mickey Mouse leer down at us from the walls. I suppress a shudder.

Xander struggles to sit up. "Did they leave any of those scalpels around?"

I look around the room. Everything is white and smells of bleach. Hospitals make my eyes and nose hurt. "I don't see one. Why?"

"All right, I guess we'll have to do it the old-fashioned way." He pulls the pillow out from behind his back and hands it to me. "Please smother me so I can be freed of this cruel world."

"Can you save the melodramatics for when Mom comes?" I yawn and shift my butt on the uncomfortable chair. "How about I find you a pen and we can ask the cute nurse to be the first one to sign your cast?"

"UGH!" Xander buries his face in his hands. "I can't believe this!"

"Let's look on the bright side," I say. "You get some sick painkillers. You'll probably get to stay home from school for the first few days. And your toes are a cool shade of purple!" I put my face right beside his puffy toes, which stick out pathetically from the huge cast wrapped around his entire left leg.

Xander makes the most pathetic sigh-hiccup I've ever heard, and I'm afraid he's about to start crying. The only time I've ever seen Xander cry was when Dad left twelve years ago. That was the last time I cried, too. There's just no point to it.

I twist uncomfortably in my seat.

"Al," he says, his voice cracking and his eyes red, "this was my one shot. My only shot to do something great."

"This isn't it," I say, staring at his hand. A part of me thinks I should hold it, or crawl into bed beside him, like I did when we were little. I opt for awkwardly avoiding eye contact instead. "When you're healed—"

"You heard the nurse. It'll be the whole season before I'm able to play. And do you really think Coach Zabinski is going to let me on the ice for playoffs if I haven't played in seven months? I barely made the team, as is."

"Ugh." I collapse back into the chair. "I know. I kicked your ass out there."

"Hey." Xander's eyebrows lower. "This is my pity party."

I watch Xander bite the corner of his left lip, and notice I'm doing the exact same thing, too. A nervous tic. "If only I could play for you," I groan.

"Yeah," Xander laughs. "Just cut your hair, why don't 'cha?"

We both laugh, and then in an instant, stare at each other with an intensity that only twins could muster. It used to freak our Mom out when we did this as kids. Mind-melding, she would call it.

"What if Xander Bell didn't break his leg?" I whisper.

"I could still have my shot," he whispers back.

I look around the room —there's just one other family soothing a bratty kid whining about his broken arm. But you never know. They could be Zabinski spies.

I draw the curtains around us. "I could play for you."

He narrows his eyes. "What do you mean?"

I move in closer, and lower my voice, even though the kid is crying so loud no one could overhear us. But I'm pretty sure it's mandatory to lower your voice when plotting a deception like this. "I'll *be* you."

"What about the little pesky fact that you're a *girl*?"

The idea erupts inside of me, as if my thoughts are the breakaway and Xander is the net I need to score in. "Coach didn't even realize I was a girl until I took my helmet off. I can cut my hair. I'll wear your clothes. We already walk, talk, and act the same. I'll get *you* noticed by the scouts. And then we can just switch back once your leg gets better."

"They'll know," he groans.

"You know they won't," I spit back. "My own boyfriend can't tell us apart when we're on the ice!"

"Oh yeah," Xander says, rubbing his chin. "He grabbed my ass once. That was awkward."

"So," I say, a smirk running the length of my face, "what do you say?"

Xander looks down. "It's too risky."

I snatch his hand, and look at him, his face more familiar than my own reflection in a mirror. "You said it yourself, Xander. This is our big break. As a family. Let me do this for you."

He looks down and bites the corner of his left lip. "Just… just don't be *too* good. Promise?"

A rush of excitement takes over my body. "Promise."

Chapter Three

It's Monday afternoon and the Falcons' first practice is tonight. We can't put this off any longer. We've set up all the details, but I can't say I'm feeling confident. But none of that little stuff — like making sure everyone thinks I'm a dude — matters right now, because tonight I GET TO PLAY HOCKEY!

Xander should be home from theater club any moment, and then the transformation will begin.

I run a hand through my long hair. When I tilt my head back, it grazes the small of my back. Mom would never let me cut it, and I'm not about to start the meltdown of the century by showing her my new 'do. So I bought enough hair extensions to make Rapunzel jealous. It'll be annoying to wear them around the house all the time, but Mom can never know about this plan. She'd never, in a million years, go along with me pretending to be a boy.

My door creaks open and Xander pokes his head in. "Hey."

"You're late. Practice starts in an hour."

"Yeah, well, I got help." Xander pushes the door open and hobbles into my room on his crutches. Behind him, a girl walks in, hefting a duffle bag larger than she is.

My heart whips into my throat. Xander doesn't bring girls home on a good day—why would he bring a stranger here, on today of all days?

"Al," Xander says, collapsing like a dying bird on my bed, "this is—"

"I'm Madison Myong!" The girl drops the giant duffel bag with a room-shaking bang and runs over to me. She snatches my hand and stares at me with shining brown eyes. "Oh my goodness. You really do look JUST like your brother."

"Uh, thanks," I say, not sure if I should take that as a compliment or not.

Madison is quite a bit shorter than me, with long silky black hair, and more makeup than face. She grabs a strand of my hair and furrows her brow. "Hmm, we'll need to get you some styling gel...and let's see what we're working with under here."

"Xander?" I squeak, as this weird girl pushes me down on the bed and starts attempting to take off my hoodie. "Can you explain what's going on?"

"Madison and I are in the theater club," he says, purposely avoiding eye contact with me. I swat Madison's hands away and she glares. "She was pretty concerned when I showed up with my broken leg—"

"Figuring he's the newest player for the Falcons and I'm their newest volunteer!" She bats her eyes, and I can hardly control rolling mine.

"Volunteer?"

"I'm trying to get into med school, so I scored a volunteer placement under the Falcons' trainers." She flips her long locks behind her head and stares off dreamily. "Isn't it so much better to be bandaging up sexy, sweaty hockey players than assessing old people's skin?" She looks down at me. "Although you weren't exactly what I had in mind."

Blood rushes through my ears. Our secret could be out before the season even begins.

"Oh, don't worry," Madison says, and places a hand on my shoulder. Can she feel me shaking? "Your secret's safe with me. I think it's amazing what you're doing. We girls got to stick together!"

I turn to Xander, and he just shrugs.

"I'll be your ally off the ice," she continues and gives a girlish giggle. "I feel like we're in a Korean drama! Isn't it to die for?"

I flop on the bed. "I wish."

"All right, hoodie off!" she squeals. "Gotta bind those boobies!"

Xander turns to the wall, and I begrudgingly comply. It's not like there's a lot to hide anyway. Madison pulls a roll of medical tape out of her bag and constricts my chest with her magic boobie-be-gone tape. I take a laboured breath as she finishes and stand in front of the mirror. Flat as a board. As I'm planning to arrive to practice with all my gear already on, no one will be able to tell a thing.

"Tip number one," Madison says, handing me a shirt, "don't go around blushing around all the players. Guys don't notice other guys' rippling pectorals and muscular abdominals..." She trails off, as if she's imagining it right now, but Xander and I just turn to each other and laugh.

"What?" Madison says.

"Trust me," Xander snorts, "that won't be a problem for Alice."

"What, are you, like, into girls?"

"No," I say, still reeling from the ridiculousness of it all. "Hockey players are just, like, the most non-sexual men out there. They're not like hot, or sexy, or whatever. They've always just been my teammates. Even when I was on the same team as Freddy..."

I trail off and turn to Xander. Shit. We didn't consider Freddy in any of this. I've been so caught up in figuring out how I was going to play in the league, I'd completely forgot about who already plays for it.

"Wait," Madison says, "who's Freddy?"

"Alice's boyfriend," Xander says. "Galen Fredlund. We call him Freddy. He plays for the Detroit Ice Wolves."

"You're dating Galen Fredlund of the *Ice Wolves*?" Madison shrieks, and I swear my windows crack.

"Uh, yeah," I say, feeling like I just announced I'm dating Hitler or something.

"The Ice Wolves are the Falcons' biggest rivals! And Fredlund...well, he's just — are you going to tell him?"

"No," I say, firm and immediate. I'm not sure when I decided that, whether it was right now or days ago, but it feels right. "This isn't my secret to tell anyone. I only see Freddy once a month anyways. On the ice, he'll just think I'm Xander."

"He never was the sharpest blade, was he?" Xander says, smirking.

Xander's never been Freddy's number one fan, but he loves me enough to try. Being with Freddy is great; I don't know if anyone else would understand my love of hockey, my commitment to going to the rink every day. And I'm always there for him too. I didn't cry or complain when Freddy got chosen to play for the Ice Wolves last year. Detroit wasn't far from our little suburb, and now with me in Chicago, I haven't found long-distance too hard.

No, we might not have the mushy lovey-dovey romance that happens in Xander's plays, but we understand each other. What more could I ask for?

I shake my head and stand. Forty-five minutes until practice.

"All right," I say, "so the three of us...we're in on this together."

Xander turns back around, and Madison gives a little hop of glee. She reaches into the duffel bag and pulls out a pair of scissors. A sadistic smile crawls up her face. "Okay," she says, snapping the scissors back and forth. "Ready for the fun part?"

"Can I?" I take the scissors from her hand and walk to the dresser mirror. I hold the metal up by my ear, catching a chunk of hair between the blades. One snip, and that's it. The decision is made.

Until Xander heals, I won't just be Alice anymore.

"You okay, Alice?" Madison whispers.

Snip.

"Call me Al."

. . .

HAYDEN

I shrug my hockey bag over my shoulder. First practice with the Falcons today. I should be excited. I mean, I am excited! But there's been this weird nervousness hanging around me all day.

Coach is going to announce the captain at practice. I don't need to worry. I know it'll be me. Who else could lead this team of schmucks? But I've been waiting for the "C" for over a year. And now that I'm finally going to get it, the only thing I can think is that I will never be as good a captain as Kevin.

I can't keep thinking like that. I clench my fists. All the coaches and trainers ever rattle on about is the power of positive thinking. Sometimes that seems harder than all the drills and sprints.

As soon as I step into the locker room, my nerves wash away as I see the familiar faces. A sense of calm rushes through me as I clap the boys on their backs and ask about their summers. All up to no good, same as usual. There are a couple of rookies wandering around, wet noodles of anxiety and nerves. Maybe I felt like that on my first day, but I definitely didn't let anyone know it. Maybe if they're lucky, I'll remember their names by the end of the season.

But there's one rookie who catches my eye, and I can't look away.

It's just so goddamn painful—like witnessing a car crash in slow motion. Most of us are half-dressed or getting ready, but this one rookie has all his gear on already, even his gloves. He's going from person to person...introducing himself?

He stands in front of Evans now. And—of course, because it's Tyler Evans—he's giving the rookie his full attention.

"Name's Alexander! But my friends call me Al."

I've only seen this guy for about two seconds, but already I'm finding it hard to believe he has any friends.

He continues to saunter from person to person, holding his glove out to greet everyone, and continues his cringe crusade. "'Sup, bro. How's it hanging? You can call me Al. Fist bump! Nah? That's cool. Super *chill*, dude. Just one of the team."

I walk to my hook and throw off my shirt. Maybe the NHL weeds out weirdos like this. I can hardly wait to get there. I feel a presence behind me.

My turn to endure the torment of this insufferable rookie.

"Hey!" he says from behind me. His voice is nasally, almost like he's got a premature cold. "I'm Alexander, but you can call—"

I turn around, and miraculously for the first time in five minutes, his chatter stops, and he just stands there, looking at me.

Creepy.

He's shorter than me even in skates. And so small, it makes me wonder why Coach let him on the team.

Okay, this is getting weird. "How about we call you what

you are?" I cross my arms over my chest. "A rookie."

• • •

ALICE

Now would be a super awesome time for me to think. I don't know how long it's been since I stopped talking, but half a billion years would be a pretty accurate guess.

It feels like there are a million things competing in my brain right now, but none of them have a chance. My visual sensory system is overloaded right now, with this guy standing in front of me.

He stares down at me, and his eyes are so brown, they're nearly black. Like his eyes are black holes, and I'm just a pathetic little asteroid, in the path of being crushed by his gravity. His hair is dark and wavy, a few strands falling over his heavy eyebrows. I trace the rest of his face with my eyes. He has a slightly crooked nose. I wonder how he broke it — a fight? Face to the boards? His mouth is long and frowning, but it wouldn't be hard to imagine a smile there.

My eyes trickle their way lower and I feel my heart bump hard against my rib cage. He's not wearing a shirt.

What is this?

This isn't me. This isn't me at all. I've always played on the boy's team and never felt this way about teammates! Even shirtless teammates.

So why is my heart fluttering, and my face on fire, and my mind empty of coherent thought? Why am I feeling like such a *girl?*

This is just dumb, inconvenient attraction. Which is definitely not okay, because I have a boyfriend! I just somehow lost all my thoughts when this guy turned around. I need to get them back, because I was doing a real great job of bonding with everyone and being a dude before I walked up to this loser.

But it's just so hard to remember how to sound like a guy when he's looking at me like that.

Then it hits me. This just isn't any teammate. This is Hayden Tremblay, the star of the Falcons. I've read about him. He moved here from Winnipeg, Manitoba when his brother, Kevin Tremblay, was drafted to Chicago's NHL team. Word has it Hayden had all the NHL scouts saying his name...until he was suspended five games last season and cost the Falcons the playoffs. Maybe that's why he looks so mad.

Coach Z's voice shocks me back to the present: "All right, boys, hit the ice!"

• • •

HAYDEN

Once I'm on the ice, I can forget about everything else... including that crazy new rookie. He's so much shorter than everyone, I can't even fathom how he got on the team. I bet Coach will cut him after a few games.

Coach starts us off doing basic drills and warming us up. It's so easy to fall back into routine. Surprisingly, most of the rookies are doing all right, even crazy number 44.

But when's Coach going to announce the new captain? After the practice? Will he have my new jersey ready?

Coach breaks us up into two teams for the last part of practice. All right, time to let the rookies know who they're playing with and remind the other guys why I'm getting the C.

As soon as the puck drops, it's like I'm in a league of my own. I win the faceoff, scoot down the ice, pass to Sacs, and now I'm lined up in front of the net. Sacs passes to me, and I pull my stick back for an easy goal.

My stick meets empty ice... The puck is gone!

I turn around, and it's that damn rookie.

Bell. Number 44.

Al.

And he's already halfway down the ice... How is he so fast? I sprint toward the other side, but he scores a goal before I make it to the blue line.

He turns around, grinning like an idiot, then skates up to me. He's hardly panting.

"Y'know," he says, "if you didn't take your eyes off the puck, I wouldn't have been able to steal it from you so easily."

I grind my teeth together. "What?"

"You took your eyes off the puck," he says slower, as if I didn't hear him the first time.

This rookie...this rookie is trying to give me advice? A hiss escapes my lips. "Don't you know who I am?"

"Yeah," he says. "You're someone who lost the puck."

• • •

Coach Zabinski blows his whistle and motions for us to huddle up. That Bell is lucky; otherwise I would have destroyed him. Who does he think he is, giving *me* advice?

That stupid rookie is going to see he didn't just mess with the best player on the Falcons. He messed with his captain.

"Nice hustle out there everyone," Coach Z says, his nose and cheeks bright red from the rink. "I like what I'm seeing, but we still have a long way to go if we're going to be any competition for the Ice Wolves."

I can't listen to Coach going on about the upcoming schedule and areas of improvement—I close my eyes and picture bringing my new jersey home to Kevin tonight. He'll think it is such a big deal, crack some beers, tell Eleanor to take a picture of the two of us in our Cs.

I look down and dig my blade into the ice. It might be kind of a fun night, I guess.

"So that brings me to our last matter," Coach says. "We don't have a captain. Every team needs a captain. And we need to make sure the Falcons have the very best. You guys deserve a captain who considers the team number one, above all else. Above their own pride. A captain who plays each game for the logo on the front, not the name on the back."

Breath comes ragged from my throat. I take off my gloves, ready to shake Coach's hand.

"And right now," Coach Z says, "no one here deserves it."

I wait a beat. No one here deserves it...except for Tremblay. That's what he's going to say, right?

"So we'll re-evaluate later in the season. That's just the way the puck drops."

This cannot be happening. No one deserves it? Is he still mad I knocked a couple guys out last season? I had more points than anyone in the league, even with my suspension!

Everyone's looking at me. They're all thinking the same thing. They're stuck with the reject Tremblay. The cast-off. The one who wasn't quite good enough.

I don't look at anyone as I skate off the ice. I've faced rejection before. Even failure. But it's never felt like this. Before, I always wanted to fight back. I wanted to prove everyone wrong.

That feeling's not here now.

In fact, I don't feel anything at all.

All I can hear is that voice inside of me repeating over and over: You aren't good enough. And you never will be.

· · ·

ALICE

Everyone's looking at Hayden as he skates off the ice. I'd feel bad for the guy if he hadn't totally ignored me when I tried to offer him some friendly advice. It had just been so easy to take the puck from him. You let your guard down when you get cocky.

The coach runs a hand over his face. "All right, kids, hit the showers."

The showers!

An icy chill runs through me as we shuffle toward the locker room. Breathe. I planned this out. I just have to make it past the showers, grab my bag, and escape.

As the guys head into the showers, I avert my eyes from their pasty bods and snatch up my bag. I dart out of the locker room and turn a corner. I'm not really familiar with these hallways yet, but it's my best bet for escape.

Except I smack right into Coach Z.

"Bell?" he says, his moustache curling into a frown. "What are you doing here? Get to the showers. You smell worse than Sacachelli's locker."

"Uh, yeah, well, I was just—"

"He was looking for me." Like an angel descending from the heavens, Madison appears behind the coach. She stands in front of him, waving a piece of paper around. "Bell suffers from severe contact dermatitis. He's allergic to soap."

Coach's eyebrows meet in the middle.

"It means," Madison continues, "unless we want the only player who can steal the puck from Tremblay to break out into hives, he'll be showering in the trainer's office."

Coach shakes his head as if we've just wasted two minutes of his life, then turns and mutters, "Hey Bell, I hope there's no hard feelings with your sister. One of the women's leagues would be lucky to have her. But you know how it is."

A smug smile spreads across my face. "Oh, don't you worry, Coach. She's managing just fine."

"Glad to hear it." He looks away. "Good job today. You really played like a man out there."

"Coach," I say, "you ain't seen nothing yet."

Chapter Four

I pull up in front of the rink. When I can't sleep, when my brain feels too foggy to think, or when everything seems to be crushing down on me, I come here.

The janitors have gotten used to me being here. As long as I stay out of their way, I can use the rink as much as I want.

I like coming here late at night. It's so quiet, all I can hear is my own breath and the slice of my blades against the ice. I can really concentrate when I'm alone, when no one's watching or judging.

But my heart sinks when I walk into the arena. I'm not alone. The rink was only supposed to be booked until 11:00 p.m. tonight, and it's almost midnight.

There's a girl out there: a figure skater, twirling around and taking up the whole rink. She wears tight black pants, and a loose T-shirt. Her face is red and glistening: she must have been out here a while. Long brown hair flows down her back.

I just can't catch a break today. I lace up my skates, grab my stick and puck, and head onto the ice. Maybe I'll scare her away.

I take a couple shots at the net but can't get into the rhythm. It's not like it should be. The scrape of her skates is deafening. I turn to glare at her. She flies on the ice, jumping, skating backward, twirling, and whipping right by me. How am I supposed to concentrate with this nonsense going on?

"Hey," I say. "This side of the rink is mine, okay? So just keep your twirling over there."

She skids to a hard stop, shooting up ice. And then she skates toward me.

I find myself inching away as she approaches. She's actually beautiful—but not in a typical way. She's more striking, having the kind of face you remember. Angled cheekbones, straight firm brows, and big autumn gray eyes that seem to capture me in a single glance—or glare, which is how she's looking at me now.

Okay, maybe I deserve that.

She's flushed and breathing heavy, gathering her long hair around her shoulder. "Excuse me?"

And her face turns into a familiar evil cocky grin.

I've seen this face before. I saw this face *this morning*. "Do I know you?"

She comes even closer with a little twirl. "Do you play for the Falcons?"

"Yeah."

"You probably know my twin brother, Al. I'm Alice."

"Yeah well, I haven't got too familiar," I say. "Rookies get cut all the time, so tell your brother not to get comfortable.'

Twin brother. That makes sense. A wave of hate flows through my body now, and I'm angry I ever thought this girl was pretty.

"You know," Alice says, grabbing my stick from me, "I

heard people say that he might break the scoring record this year."

I cross my arms. "Yeah, what people?"

"Just people." She smirks the same smirk that punk gave me earlier. She pulls the stick back and shoots the puck. It misses the net by a mile, but she's not even holding the stick properly. She shrugs. "I've never been good at hockey."

"Must run in the fam—"

"Not like my brother." She interrupts me. "They say he might even be better than Tremblay. That Hayden's all hype, no actual follow through."

She drops the stick and it clatters to the ice. A dark shadow trails her as she circles me then skates off the ice. "See you around. Maybe at one of my brother's games."

I don't say anything, just watch as she sashays away. Finally, I find the words and shout: "Not if I see you first!"

But she's already gone.

• • •

ALICE

It's no wonder so many talented players choke when it's game time. There's so much stimuli: the roaring crowd, the sea of royal blue jerseys with the soaring white falcon, the red flash of the timer on the screen. If you let all that outside stuff get to you, you can't concentrate on the only thing that matters: the puck.

Of course, there is one sensation I can't help noticing. I shift my weight from one butt cheek to the other, and wonder if I can rub my numb ass without anyone noticing. Although, maybe that would be considered a guy-ish thing to do.

I've been sitting on this damn bench the majority of the game. I'm not too bummed; as a rookie, I can't expect much ice time until I prove myself. And I'm working on it. I already got an assist on Hayden Tremblay's goal last period. Who knows what other magic I could have created out there? Unfortunately, Hayden refuses to pass to me. Maybe he's mad about what "Alice" said to him last night. I just couldn't help myself — he needs to be taken down a peg, or fifty.

Either way, we're down a goal in the third period, and there's only two minutes left.

Coach Z whacks me on the back. "Tremblay, Bell, get out there. Let's see you score another one."

I jerk at the sound of my name. Two minutes left and Coach is putting me in? He must really be desperate. I jump over the boards and skate to the middle of the rink.

Hayden is a centre, so he's in position to take the faceoff. I'm a right-winger — a goal scorer, a playmaker. I steady my breathing and keep my stick on the ice. I have to shut everything out. But my eyes drift to Hayden. His jaw is set, dark eyes determined. Anger flickers in his gaze.

I've been told so many times, "It's just a game." But that's not true. Hockey has never been just a game to me—it's been my safety net, my anchor, my purpose. And the look on Hayden's face makes me think he feels the same.

The puck drops and I tear myself from space and back onto the rink. Hayden wins the puck, and I sprint down the ice, narrowly avoiding a collision with the opposing defensemen. I get into position and I'm wide open. Hayden careens toward me with the puck, and I smack my stick so he can see I'm open. He looks at me—

And shoots the puck straight at the net.

Bastard!

The goalie easily covers the puck and the ref stops play.

We skate toward the faceoff circle. "I was wide open," I say to Hayden.

He doesn't even look at me.

Another puck drops and Hayden loses. I chase the puck

toward our end. With only a minute left, we don't have time to be near our net!

I dart into the end zone to steal the puck, but an opposing player charges at me. I gasp, narrowly dodging out his way as he slams against the boards. My heart pounds in my chest. Damn, the players are aggressive. And huge. If I put myself in there, they'll be scraping pieces of me off the ice.

One of our opponents shoots the puck, and it dings off the post, sailing straight for me. Instinct takes over, and I snatch the puck up. My legs may not be as long as anyone else's, and my body might not be as big, but I'm fast. And now it's just me, with nine players struggling in my wake.

The goalie looms before me, a boulder in my path. But this is my breakaway. This is my game.

And this will be my goal.

I shoot and the puck sails straight through the goalie's five-hole.

The light goes off, the buzzer sounds, and the crowd erupts louder than anything I've ever heard before.

I scored?

I scored!

My team wraps around me, and I'm lost amidst the giants smothering me with hugs. I lean my head back, taking in the sea of royal blue jerseys on their feet.

But then I see one blue jersey skating back toward the bench. Number nine. Hayden Tremblay. I guess even forcing the game into overtime isn't enough to earn his respect.

I plop back down on the bench, feeling as if it's a throne. Coach pats my helmet. "Nice breakaway, kid."

"Thanks," I say, beaming.

Overtime slugs by—a heart pounding, goalless five minutes. And that means it's time for a shootout.

My skates tap nervously on the ground. Shootouts have always been my strong suit. My team could count on me as their clutch girl.

I look at the opposing team's goalie. I can already tell his left side is his weak point. I could get up close, deke right, then sneak it in his left side…

Coach scribbles on his clipboard; he needs to submit his three players for the shootout. "Okay, Sacachelli, Gerver, and Trem—"

"Coach." I stand up. "Put me out there. I know what to do."

I hear an audible scoff from Hayden but ignore it. Coach Z stares at me from under his bushy eyebrows then flips open his clipboard. "You got bad stats in shootouts from your last league, Bell. I don't think so."

Shit! Xander blew at shootouts, and now I'm stuck with his crappy stats. "Trust me, Coach," I plead. "Weren't you watching my breakaway? I can do this."

Hayden stands up. "Sit down, rookie. Maybe when you hit puberty, you can take a turn."

Coach flicks his eyes between us, and I can almost see the rusty wheels spinning beneath his thinning hair. "All right, Bell, you're up. Don't fuck this up."

"Are you kidding me?" Hayden roars, ripping off his helmet and throwing it to the ground.

"What makes you think I trust you to shoot," Coach says to Hayden, "if you don't know how to pass?"

Hayden looks like his head is about to fly off his shoulders. I can't help myself. I flash him the smallest of smiles.

My pride quickly turns to fear as I stare out on the ice. Coach tells us the shooting lineup: I'll be last to shoot. Maybe Sacachelli and Gerver will come through and it won't even get to me.

Heart pounding, I watch as our goalie easily stops the first shot against us. I cheer on Sacachelli as he skates out to center ice. But as soon as he picks up the puck, I can tell he'll flub the shot. His grip on the stick is too tight, his knees locked. His shot bounces harmlessly off the goalie's pads.

Three more shots to go before the game rests on my shoulders. Our goalie stops the next shot, but then Gerver rings the puck off the post. I hold my breath. If the other team scores this next shot, they win. If they don't...it's up to me.

My eyes follow the puck as it travels from our opponent's stick, flies through the air, and smashes into our goaltender's glove.

All eyes on the bench turn to me. I can practically feel the heat searing through my body from Hayden's vicious gaze.

"Get out there, Bell," Coach says. "We're counting on you."

Blood rushes to my ears, drowning out the roar of the crowd. If I score, we win the game.

I jump over the boards and as soon as my skates hit the ice, my nervousness is gone. Fear has travelled through me, leaving nothingness in its path. And I replace that nothingness with a single thought:

Score.

Sometimes I visualize what I'm going to do, and I can replicate it perfectly. Sometimes I don't know where I'll shoot the puck until I finally do it. And right now, instinct takes over. The puck is on my stick, I spin, swipe to the left, shoot...

The net lights up.

The Falcons erupt, jumping over the bench and crowding onto the ice. We embrace and high-five one another until we're all raspy voiced and exhausted. Finally, it's time to head toward the showers. Just as I'm about to leave the ice, I see the puck still lying in the net.

I scoop it up. A souvenir, from my first game with the Falcons.

I turn and skate toward the benches. There's still one player left—the only player who didn't join in the celebration.

His wavy brown hair falls over his face, but I can tell his gaze is distant.

"Hey," I say.

Hayden jumps and looks up. "What?"

I feel as if I just sprinted down the ice—my heart flutters in my chest, and I can hardly breathe. "Uh, I just..." I clear my throat, and make sure to deepen my voice a few octaves, like Xander taught me to. "I, uh, just thought you might want the game-winning puck. We couldn't have done it without you."

Slowly, Hayden reaches out and takes the puck. He twirls it between his fingers—then whips it across the rink. It smashes against the boards.

"Just stay out of my way," he sneers and storms toward the locker room.

I wait until I can no longer see number nine to throw my head back and open my mouth as loud as I can. I want to scream, but I haven't practiced my boy scream yet, so it would probably come out too girly.

Screw Hayden Tremblay. I've tried to be nice, but I'm the one who scored the tying goal and won the shootout. Heck, he won't even pass to me. From now on, Tremblay better stay out of my way.

Chapter Five

It's been twenty-four hours since I killed it at yesterday's game, but I'm still beaming. It doesn't matter that I had to wake up an hour early for school to clip my extensions in, and it certainly doesn't matter that Hayden Tremblay hates me—I'm on top of the world!

"Ma, watch this!" I call from the top of the stairs.

She looks up at me from under her thick, cat-eye glasses. "Alice, if you're about to do what I think you are—"

"Whee!" I slide down the bannister, gaining enough momentum to perform a perfect upright spin as I sail off.

Mom sighs audibly. "If only you twirled like that on the ice."

I jog into the dining room and plop down at the table. Xander was on dinner duty tonight, and there's a plethora of steaming dishes laid out. He always does a way better job cooking than I do. Of course, there's only two plates set out. I can't remember the last time Mom joined us.

Strangely enough, she's followed me into the dining room and sits down at the table.

Xander and I both look at each other. "Uh," I say, "are you eating with us?"

She wrinkles her nose as if I've just wildly offended her. "Am I not allowed?"

Hesitantly, I stand and grab an extra plate and fork from the kitchen. This is weird. She must want something.

"So, Alice," she says, raising a perfectly arched brow, "have you been practicing your figure skating for the charity events coming up?" She loves to talk in an overly posh way, as if she's doing a terrible English accent. Maybe she thinks if she over-articulates every word, her point will come across better.

"I've been really busy with school and the women's hockey team," I say, stuffing some roast beef in my mouth. "I stay late after hockey practice to go over the Ice Ball routine."

Mom sticks out her lip.

"Ah, Ma," I say. "Don't do the lip thing."

It goes out even farther.

"Look what you've done," Xander groans, the first thing he's said to me all day.

Now the lip tremble.

"What, Ma!" I cry. "I'm just so busy! I have homework and practice and classes!"

"You won't know the routine," Mom wails, and her glasses start to fog. "Don't you know how important this is to me, Alice, to the city?"

"Great job," Xander says, handing some napkins to Mom. "Ma's been working really hard on this charity Ice Ball, Al. And you've just been spending all your time playing hockey."

I shoot Xander a look. Why's he throwing me under the bus when he knows why I've been so busy?

"I've only just started this job," Mom says, amidst sniffles.

"Do you know how hard it is to come from a small town and suddenly be the head of the seventy-fourth largest non-profit in Chicago?"

I resist rolling my eyes. She'll tell me.

"Extremely hard!" Mom blows her nose into one of the napkins. "And I've been working day and night to pull off this charity skate—"

I hope Ma doesn't see my eyes start to glaze over. I can't deal with this right now. Ever since I was old enough to put on skates, Mom has been trying to force me into figure skating—and I've done it every single year to shut her up.

"—and all I want is for my beautiful daughter to perform the final dance—"

How am I supposed to commit to it when there's so much work to put into the Falcons? Our first away game of the season is coming up next week, and I have to be ready.

"—I've even got the Chicago Falcons involved in a promotional event! Doesn't that make you happy?"

I'll be taking a bus to Detroit and staying in a room with another player. Pretending to be a boy on the ice is one thing, but the real challenge will be pretending full time. Although that's probably easier than dealing with all this girl crap.

"And so will you please just care about this? A little!"

"Yes, Ma!" I say, shaking my head and making eye contact. Hopefully she couldn't tell I was zoned out for that entire lecture. I stab my fork into the meat. "Can you just tell me one more time what I signed up for?"

Ma's lip recedes ever so slightly, and she sighs. "I just told you! The promotional event and the Ice Ball in the spring! I want you to skate beautifully."

"Oh yeah! Of course. I promise I'll be there!" It's only two events, I repeat in my head. I can make it through that.

A lipstick smile spreads across Mom's face. "Oh, wonderful." Her cell phone in her lap begins to buzz. "Oh my, I must take this. The trials of a working woman! Please excuse me." Mom dances off, trilling into her phone.

Xander pushes his chair away from the table and grabs his crutches.

"Where are you going?" I say, mouth full.

"Not hungry."

"Dude, what's your problem? You haven't talked to me all day. Didn't you watch the live stream of the game last night?"

"Yes, I watched it." Xander's gaze shoots through me like a slapshot. "What the hell, Alice?"

I recoil back. "What do you mean, what the hell? I scored in the shootout!"

"I know!" Xander burrows his head in his hands. "What were you thinking? What part of lay low don't you understand?"

"I don't understand," I say. "I wanted to play well. For you."

"For me?" Xander scoffs and shakes his head. "How am I supposed to replicate the way you play when I come back, huh? You're just supposed to be place holding, Alice, not stealing the show."

I lean back in my chair. "Chill out. I've got it under control."

"And now you're going away to play the Ice Wolves…" Xander can't meet my gaze.

"Why don't you come up to Detroit for the weekend? All of our old teammates will be in town. You could say hi to Freddy and Ben Walker—"

"No!" He physically recoils at the mention of it. "I just…I just want you to stay out of sight. Don't talk to the team that much. Don't show them up at games. Just…be a little less Alice, okay?"

I stand up and wrap my arms around Xander's shoulders.

"You've got nothing to worry about, baby brother," I say, nestling my head in his ear. "Because I'm not Alice. I'm Al."

• • •

The bus's roaring engine has become more of a comfort than an annoyance after the six-hour ride. I let my eye lids droop, drifting off to the choking rasp of the engine.

Sure, I've been trapped in this tin can for six hours while my teammates fart and make dumb comments about the first thing that comes into their brains, but I'm used to that. Usually it's nice to have Xander beside me on these big team rides, but my excitement is the only company I need today.

My first away game with the team is tomorrow! And it's in Detroit! And to make it even more exciting, we'll be facing the Ice Wolves—my boyfriend's team. I've gone to so many of Freddy's games, I can picture their plays in my head. It should be a piece of cake—if Hayden decides to pass to me.

I pretend to scratch my back, but actually adjust the medical tape, strapped tight around my chest like an elastic band. I'll get to see Freddy, too, so there's that. I called him last week and told him I would be in Detroit to watch Xander's game. I'll have to make sure my dress and makeup bag are well hidden so none of my teammates see.

We pull up in front of our hotel. It's a rather warm evening for October; orange leaves scatter the sidewalk.

I pull out my phone and send a text to Freddy:

Me: *Just got to the hotel. When do you want to meet up?*

Does that sound excited enough for a girl who hasn't seen her boyfriend in two months? I add a smiley face for good measure.

Freddy texts me back almost immediately:

Freddy: *wat time do u hed back to Chi-town?*

Me: *Not until the day after the game.*

Freddy: *Coach wants us to stay in n get sum rest 4 tom's game. Can we meet up after I kick ur bro's ass tomorrow?*

Me: *Sure.*

I know I shouldn't, but I can't help but add:

I'll console you after your loss.

I place my phone back in my pocket. Now what am I going to do? Coach Z hasn't put any restrictions on us, as far as I know, but I definitely don't want to spend my night awkwardly bro-bonding with whoever my roommate is. Maybe I can see what Madison's up to...

I walk into the lobby and straight into a heated argument between Hayden and Coach. Hayden shoots me the nastiest glare, and for a second, I think the argument is about me. But it can't be—I haven't done anything to him.

"*You.*"

At least I don't think I did.

"Room with Bell?" Hayden snarls, turning back to Coach. "Are you kidding me? I always room with Sacs!"

Daniel Sacachelli wraps an arm around Hayden's shoulder. "Yeah, come on, Zab. Tremblay and I have a routine."

"That's exactly why I'm separating you two." Coach shoots them each a dirty look. "No more of your shenanigans. No more raiding mini-fridges. No more parties. No more girls. And no more—" He pokes Sacachelli hard in the chest. "—punching cab drivers."

"That was one time!" Sacachelli moans.

"You two are bad influences on each other." Coach crosses his arms. "Sacachelli, you're with Evans. Tremblay, you're with Bell." He walks toward me and places the key card in my hand. "Keep him out of trouble, rookie."

I look up to give Hayden a reassuring smile, but he's already storming toward the elevator. I hike my bag up on my shoulder and hurry after him. This should be perfect; I'm pretty sure Hayden hates me, so he'll ignore me...which is all I can ask out of a roommate right now.

But my stomach shrivels up into a tight ball.

Hayden doesn't talk to me when we enter the room, so I walk past him and throw my duffle bag on the far bed.

He makes a sound in the back of his throat like I just insulted his family's honour, storms over, rips my bag off the bed and hurls it at me so hard, I tumble back onto the other bed.

"Dude, what the fuck!"

He doesn't respond. His back is to me, and he looks out the window. His hands are clenched in his hair. And I realize for the first time, maybe this isn't about me at all.

But that doesn't sit with me for long, because even if it's not, he's still being a goddamn asshole about it.

I storm over to him and clear my throat so I can summon my most powerful manly voice. "Hey!"

"I *always* sleep on the bed closest to the window." He turns around. "And I told you to stay out of my way."

"What is your problem with me?" I shout, cautious of my voice going up an octave.

"You ruin everything! On the ice—" He cuts himself off. On the ice, he has to work a little harder to keep the puck now that I'm here. But there's no way in hell that he's going to admit that out loud.

Someone pounds on our door and a bunch of rowdy voices jeer outside. I guess our bickering will have to wait.

Hayden goes to the door and Daniel Sacachelli, Tyler Evans, and some other boys file in the room. They've all got their coats, hats, gloves, and scarves on.

"You ready, man?" Daniel says, looking at Hayden.

"Yeah, give me a minute." He grabs his bag and fishes out a jacket.

"You coming, rookie?" Tyler says, looking at me with a big smile. I've decided I really like Tyler. I'd razz him for being obnoxiously happy, but he's just so genuine.

"Going where?" I take a step back. I'm hardly ever around these guys without skates and suddenly I feel really small. I smooth out my long-sleeve blazer—one of several outfit options Xander gave me. Without my helmet and jersey, I feel so exposed. Can they see the softness of my jaw? My narrow shoulders? Can't they hear it in my voice?

"There's always a bonfire the night before the big game," Tyler says. "We go every year. You should come."

It does sound sorta fun, but it wouldn't really classify in Xander's book as keeping my head down.

"No thanks," I mutter. "I'm pretty tired."

"Probably a good thing. Don't want to show the Ice Wolves what a small fry we got on the team now," Daniel says, pushing me in the elbow. He's got an easy grin on his face, and I know he's just teasing.

Normally, I'd shoot him a witty comeback. But his words are still making their way through my head and all that comes out is: "The Ice Wolves are going to be there?"

"Unfortunately," Tyler says. "They always put on a bonfire the night before we play them, to try and psyche us out by talking shit. Doesn't work for us though! We just go and steal their beer."

But…Freddy said their coach told them to stay in. That can't be right.

"Comin', Al?" Daniel looks back as they all start filing

out the door.

"Yeah, wait for me!"

"Great," Hayden throws his head back and moans. "My agony continues."

I reach for my knit cap and the biggest jacket I own. Anger pinches in my belly. Why would Freddy lie to me? Maybe the Ice Wolves are disobeying their coach. But Freddy wouldn't do that.

Heat rises to my face. Sure, Freddy's been known to skip a practice or two in favor of sleeping off a hangover. But he's always told me. And we haven't seen each other in two months. Why wouldn't he want me there?

I set my jaw. Freddy wouldn't lie to me, so there's no way he'll be at this bonfire.

But I better go just to make sure.

• • •

HAYDEN

"And don't even get me started on the way he does his shootouts." I take a sip of my beer and look up. "Hey, where did Sacs go?"

Evans gives me a pained grin. "He left when you started talking about the way Bell chews on his mouthguard."

"Well, it's stupid! Mouth guards are supposed to be in your mouth—not chewed on when you're about to score a goal." I lean against a table and look around the bonfire. The Wolves set it up on the outskirts of the city, in one of the player's giant backyard. There's a big fire in the middle, surrounded by camp chairs and bales of hay.

There's about fifty people here, drinking, laughing, doing dumb stuff. I find Sacs in the crowd. He's found a group of pretty girls. Normally I would be right there with him, but there's too much annoyance simmering inside me.

I turn back to Evans, and his blond hair glows orange in the firelight. At least he's still my friend.

"I just don't understand why Coach even put him on the team." I glance at Bell, who stands alone on the outskirts of the bonfire, dressed in a jacket more suited for a blizzard than a party. "And have you noticed the way—"

"NO!" Evans snatches the empty can out of my hand. "I haven't noticed! Hayden, I know you love to obsess over *everything*—your workouts, diet, practices—but I've never seen you obsess over another player." He shoves a beer in my gaping hand. "So what if Coach put him in the shootout instead of you? He's a good player. We should be happy he's on the team." Evans swigs his drink. "Now I'm going to rescue that poor girl from Sac's horrible pickup lines, because if I have to hear one more complaint about Al Bell, I will personally throw myself in the fire."

I down my drink and toss my empty cup on the table. Obsessed with Bell? Hardly. Yeah, other players have riled me up before... Okay, a lot of players have. But no player has ever gotten quite under my skin the way Bell has.

I hate everything about him. I hate that he's so small, he shouldn't even be able to play hockey. I hate how he can deke around the players so fast, no one can catch him. I hate the way he talks like his nose is always stuffed. Even his sister is annoying.

And why the hell is he standing so far away from everyone? Way to be a team player. Before I know it, I walk toward him to see what the unsociable loser is up to.

Bell looks up at me when I get there. "So," he says, "I guess it's true all Canadians wear plaid."

I look down at my plaid jacket and wonder if he's trying to be funny. "Eh?"

"Eh!" He laughs as if I've said something hysterical. "Have you come over to say sorry, too?"

I cross my arms. Maybe it's the beer, or maybe its just cause he's so damn pathetic right now, but my anger from earlier is gone.

He gives me a sideway glance, almost like he expects me to hurl an insult his way. I grab him by the arm and pull him toward the fire. "Don't stand out in the shadows like a weirdo. You'll give the Falcons a bad name."

Bell reluctantly trails behind me. Something is up. He's usually super chatty—to an uncomfortable extreme. But he turns dead quiet, his eyes darting around. "You used to live around here, didn't you?" I ask. "You know any of these guys?"

"I never told you that."

Shit. Well, obviously I had to creep his hockey history. How a kid I've never heard of suddenly made it on the Falcons—and is good enough to take the puck from me— that's something I have to find out. And my background research on him doesn't turn anything up. Bell played in a small town local league, and his stats were average at best. "Uh…" I pull my toque further down. "It's important for me to know about my teammates."

"Because you want to be captain?"

"I never told you that." I look down at him. Usually when people bring up the C, I get defensive, but there's something about the way he asks. It's not an accusation, and that makes it feel all right.

Bell shrugs and looks around again. "I know one guy, but I don't think he's here. Galen Fredlund."

I laugh. "How do you know an asshole like that?"

"Uh…" He shoves his hands in his pockets. "My twin sister's dating him."

I squint my eyes. Why would that hot figure skater be dating an asshole like Galen Fredlund? "I saw him earlier."

"He's here?"

"Yeah, on the other side of the fire."

Suddenly, Bell moves so fast, I have to jog to keep up with him. When I make it around the fire, Bell has stopped completely, staring at Fred. The asshole is sitting on a hay bale, surrounded by a pack of Ice Wolves. On his lap sits some blonde girl, wearing a dress that can't be keeping her warm at all. Not that Fred's letting her get cold with his tongue down her throat and his hands on her ass.

Bell rushes forward.

Fuck. He'll get his ass kicked if he calls out Fredlund right now.

"Al, wait!" I grab his arm, and he spins around.

"Fuck, I'm Al—" he mutters to himself. His hands clench at his side, and his face is twisted in indecision. Or constipation...I can't really tell.

I'm not one to ever back down from a fight, but Bell's half the size of Fred, and there's a bunch of his dipshit friends around. Bell gives me a nod, and we start to walk away.

"Xander?!"

I turn around and Fredlund stands up, pushing the blonde off his lap. Bell hasn't turned around; he grabs the corners of his toque, pulls it down over his ears, and mutters something. Then he clears his throat and charges toward Fred.

"What the fuck are you doing?" Bell roars.

Fredlund squints. He wavers on his feet, clearly drunk out of his mind. "Xander? How in the hell did *you* make it on the Falcons? Good for you, man." He tries to hug him, but Bell dodges out of the way.

"What the hell is wrong with you? What about Alice?" Pain is etched across his face.

Fredlund runs a hand through his blond curls. I guess he just realized he's not gonna be all buddy-buddy with Bell after cheating on his sister. Idiot.

"Look," he mutters, looking down. "You know how it is,

man."

"No! I don't know how it is! And neither does Alice!"

Fredlund's eyes go wide. "Alice knows I love her. Jesus, she lives so far away, we barely see each other, and even when we do...you know how she is. "

"Yeah, I do know how she is. She wouldn't put up with your shit, so you found someone who would. I get it!" Bell turns to leave, but Fredlund reaches forward and roughly grabs the hood of his jacket.

"Fuck that, Xander," Fredlund says. "Don't you fucking act like you have morals! Just cover for me one more time."

Bell breaks free of Fredlund's grasp. "C-cover?"

"You heard me!" Fred grabs Bell by the arm, pulls him close, and whispers something in his ear. Bell's eyes go wide, and Fredlund pushes him away. "You think I'm joking, Xander?"

Anger bubbles in my chest. Sure, Alice was annoying, but she doesn't deserve this. I can't take this asshole anymore!

I walk forward and yank Bell away from Freddy's grip. Fredlund looks at me for one confused moment, before I pull back my fist and punch him in the mug.

He staggers back, clutching his nose and screaming. Luckily, he's too drunk to fight—but his friends aren't. I glance down at Bell. "Wanna get outta here?"

Bell nods, and we sprint onto the road. The streetlights stream over us as we dart away, listening to the jeers and laughing die away behind us. Finally, when we're deep into the suburbs of nowhere, and the party is long behind us, we stop running.

Bell bends over panting. Finally, he looks up at me and mumbles, "Why did you do that for me? You don't even like me."

I throw a hand behind my head and look away. "You're a part of the Falcons. And nobody messes with my team."

...

ALICE

"I'm so full I'm going to die." I clutch my stomach and look down at my empty pizza tray.

Hayden looks over at me, wide-eyed. "You just ate a whole pizza. Honestly, where do you put it all?"

I grab the dessert menu off the table. I thought being a guy would make people stop questioning how much I eat.

"You're getting dessert, too?"

"My dinner stomach is full, but my dessert stomach has room." After Hayden punched Freddy in the nose, we walked into the city and ended up at this dive pizza shop, claiming to have Detroit's best pizza.

And y'know...I think they might be right.

I stare at Hayden, rattling off about how pie is the only worthy dessert. Despite him being a complete asshole 90% of the time, I can't deny how nice his voice is. It's deep, with that unique Canadian twang. I wonder if everyone from Winnipeg talks like he does.

"So, did you tell your sister about Fredlund?"

Ugh. Freddy. There's a part of me that just wants to crawl onto the linoleum of this pizza joint and die. But there's another part that just wants to eat a huge slab of cheesecake and call it a night. Freddy and I dated for two years. And there were a lot of good times. But now that I think about it, we spent a good chunk of those two years either playing hockey or ignoring the other. He moved on.

Would have been nice if he had just broke up with me first.

I know I should be holding back tears, but there's just none in me. I don't think I could shed a single tear even if my life depended on it. All my tears left when Dad did.

"Bell?"

"What?" Oh yeah. He asked me about Freddy. "I haven't told her yet. I'll do it in person."

I want to text Freddy, tell him it's over, and that he's an asshole. But I can't do that, not without talking to Xander first. Because when Freddy pulled me close, he had whispered: *If you tell Alice, I'll tell your secret to the whole league.*

What secret? Xander doesn't have secrets...and I would know. I'm his twin! But has Freddy been blackmailing Xander? And did Xander know Freddy was cheating on me?

My body goes cold thinking about it.

"So, Xander? Should we all be calling you that?"

"No," I say a little too harshly. "It's just a stupid nickname from back home."

"Hey, you okay?" Hayden gives me a strange look. If I didn't know better, I might even say he looks concerned.

"Yeah...just thinking about Alice."

Hayden sighs. "It blows, but she's better off without him. Fredlund is a total asshole—on and off the ice."

"Really?"

"Yeah," Hayden says. "He's a huge reason we hate the Ice Wolves. He's a straight-up goon. Gets in fights almost every game. And sure, I do that, too, but only if someone knocks down one of my guys. Fred goes for anyone without reason. And he gets right personal with you, in the worst ways." Hayden runs a hand through his wavy hair. "And what he did today—total dick move."

"I know!" I say, feeling so justified in my anger. "I would never do that to him—" I trail off and catch myself. "To my girlfriend."

"You have a girlfriend?" Hayden sounds surprised.

"Uh no, but if I did." And then because I can't help myself, I ask, "What about you?"

Hayden chuckles. "Hah. No girlfriend."

Okay. I get it. No girlfriend, but *girlfriends*. I shouldn't be surprised...just look at him! With his stupid accent, and plaid clothing, and brown tousled hair...he could win Mr. Lumberjack, or whatever.

"Why?" he says, smirking. "Trying to set me up with your sister?"

I jerk forward. "No!"

He laughs. "Chill, Bell. I don't have a sister, but if I did, I sure as hell wouldn't want her dating a guy like me."

• • •

We walk back to the hotel, and the cold breeze is heaven on my flushed face. Hayden and I don't talk, but it's an easy silence. It feels like we've agreed on a truce tonight, and I don't want it to end.

"Hey, Hayden," I mutter once we get in view of the hotel.

"Yeah."

"Since you've decided not to hate me..."

"Who said I decided not to hate you?" he says, but a smile creeps up his face.

"Well, you punched Freddy in the face for me, and we ate pizza together, so I think that means we're obligatory friends now."

He pushes me on the shoulder. "I punched Freddy in the face for your sister, and because you're on my team...but go on."

"I really want to...no, I *need* to win tomorrow. So...think you can pass me the puck?"

"What?"

"On the ice!" I say, looking up at him. Come on, he can't *not* realize he's been thwarting me every single game. "Just work with me!"

"Creaming Fred and his little puppies would be sweet."

He gives me a sideways glance. "But the Ice Wolves are a rough team. You ready to play hard against them?"

Honestly, I've never been so ready for anything in my entire life. I stick out my hand. "A truce to beat the Ice Wolves?"

Hayden raises his heavy eyebrows. Then his face cracks, and he takes my hand. "A truce to beat the Ice Wolves."

Chapter Six

I blink sweat out of my eyes and focus on my heavy breathing to drown out the roar of the crowd. Ice Wolves fans are never the most welcoming to us, especially when we're leading 3-1. Now there's five minutes left in the third, but I know every minute counts.

Fredlund flies down the ice with the puck, darting through our defense. Dammit! He may be the hugest asshole on the planet, but he can be dangerous with that puck. Now it's just him and our goalie—I can almost hear the buzzer ringing in my head.

Suddenly, Bell appears out of nowhere. He drags his stick, whizzes to the right—and takes off with the puck. I blink dumbly for a few seconds before I get my ass in gear and hightail it to the deep-end. Bell passes it to me, and the net gapes open.

But Bell's quicker than I am and already in position. His gaze meets mine—an electric shock. I could take the shot from here… Instead, I pass and the puck sails across the ice, hitting Bell's stick square in the centre.

He shoots and…the light flashes! The buzzer goes off! Another goal for Tremblay and Bell!

My teammates crowd around me, and I relish every second, every pat on the back, every hack-eyed grin. But I look through the sea of jerseys for number forty-four. Bell stands on the outskirts of our huddle, giving me a stupid grin.

I fight my way out of a sea of gloves and bodies and swing an arm around Bell. "Not a bad goal, rookie."

"Yeah," he says, looking away from me. "It was an all right pass."

I laugh. Bell and I have been on fire tonight. Every time I needed the puck, he was right there to pass to me. And every time I set up a play, it's like he was reading my mind, skating exactly where I needed him to be. I guess I may have discredited him before—

Suddenly, Bell's jerked out from under my arm. At first, I think it's another one of the boys congratulating him on his goal, but then I see the bright turquoise flash of an Ice Wolves jersey.

"What the fuck, Xander?" Fredlund has Bell by the jersey, his face bursting with sweat and veins, like an angry red blister, ready to pop. "What kind of shit are you trying to pull?"

Bell's face drains of color, and I can see the white all around his eyes. Fredlund towers over him, the bulk of his body enshrouding Bell in shadow. Fredlund pulls back his fist and Bell shuts his eyes.

In a single instant, I body slam Fredlund, tearing Bell out of his grip. I catch my balance then draw my arm back, pounding away at his smug face.

"Hayden!" a high-pitched voice screeches, and Bell yanks me back. The whole team descends on us, and the refs fight their way in, one grabbing my arm, and the other with a hand on Fredlund's shoulder. He wipes his bloody nose and stares at Bell.

"Don't fuck things up for me, Xander," he snarls. "You wouldn't want your secret getting out to the whole league."

Bell stares blankly, then turns away.

Once we're all separated, the refs dole out penalties. Bell and I sit together in the penalty box.

"What am I even doing in here?" Bell groans. "I didn't start anything."

"Fredlund really hates you."

"Yeah." His mouth guard dangles from the corner of his mouth. "Uh, so thanks for that. Coach's going to kill you for getting in another fight."

I look over at Coach Z, who just nods at me. "I think this time he might make an exception."

Bell looks up at me. "Why's that?"

A smile crosses my face. "Maybe this time, I found the right reason to fight."

Bell must still be out of breath, as his face turns a billion shades of red. I hand him the water bottle.

"So how'd you know how to steal the puck from Fredlund back there?" I say.

"Oh, uh, it was pretty easy to tell what he was gonna do," Bell says, scratching his skate against the ground. "I taught him that move."

"Hah!" I throw my head back and laugh. "You would have thought he'd have remembered that! Well, you did good, Bell. You stayed pretty calm when Fred was going apeshit at you."

Bell doesn't say anything for a long time. I flick my eyes away from him and stare at the penalty timer, slowly ticking down the seconds.

"I just," Bell finally says, his voice almost a squeak,

"didn't want to fight him."

"You gotta fight eventually," I say. The penalty timer finally runs out, and we stand. "Maybe I have a few things to teach you, Bell."

Bell raises an eyebrow. "Yeah, well maybe I have a few things to teach you, too." He jumps onto the ice.

"Hey!" I call, and he looks back at me. "What was Fredlund talking about earlier? About your secret?"

Bell touches his chest with his glove. "Me? I don't have any secrets."

Chapter Seven

ALICE

The day I get home from Detroit, I'm a mess of nerves. I pace around my bedroom, then up and down the stairs, go to the kitchen and make a sandwich but can't eat. I go back to my bedroom, open my duffel bag to unpack, but it's like I've forgotten where everything goes.

I need to talk to Xander. I need to know what this secret is.

My pulse roars in my ears: I wish I could just go to the rink and skate all this anxiety out. Everything makes sense on the ice. When did my life become so complicated? How did Hayden Tremblay become the good guy and Xander the bad one?

I throw myself on my bed and bury my head under the pillows. Maybe if I take a long enough nap, all of my problems will have just disappeared when I wake up—

"Hey, you feeling okay?"

I turn to see Xander sticking his head through the

doorway. My mouth is dry, and I can't even say hello.

"Did everything go okay in Detroit?" Xander asks cautiously.

"Yeah, we creamed the Ice Wolves." I could keep it at that, not saying anything more, and burying the memories of the bonfire as deep as I can. But instead, it's like the fire erupts within my chest, and anger and sadness well up until I have to say it. "Xander...did you know Freddy was cheating on me?"

Xander stumbles back as if I just shot an arrow into his shoulder. "W-what?"

I look down and pick at a hangnail. "We went to the Ice Wolves' bonfire the night before the game. Freddy was making out with some girl."

"I-I d-don't..." Xander stutters, then suddenly his face hardens. "What do you mean you went to the bonfire? Alice! You could have got caught!"

I stand up. "No, *you* got caught lying to me. Freddy saw me and thought I was you, obviously, and—"

"What did he say?"

I take a breath, then spill it all: Freddy's warning about Xander's secret, Hayden punching him out, and Freddy's taunt at the game.

My brother's face falls, his skin pale and eyes faraway. All the anger in me simmers down to ash. "Xander," I whisper, "I'm not mad. Just tell me what's going on so I can do something about it."

Xander stays silent for seconds that feel like years. A million thoughts go through my head: Have I said the wrong things? Should I go hug him?

Finally, he says, "There's nothing you can do, Alice. Just drop it."

"What's this secret?" I say, voice rising. "You can tell me! It's me!"

"There's no secret!" Xander snaps and turns away. "I can't believe you'd go to the bonfire... I told you to lay low!"

"Wait, so I'm the bad guy?" I say. "You lied to me..."

"It's my life you're messing with, Alice—"

"It's my life, too!"

"Just drop it!" Xander roars. He buries his face in his hands. "Alice, *please*. Just stick to the ice. Just play the damn game! That's it!"

My heart drums slow and hard in my chest. "Fine," I say quietly. "If there's no secret, then there's no reason for me to stay with Freddy. I guess I'll just break up with him."

Xander pauses in my doorway for a moment and then says, "I told you he was an asshole."

"Yup," I whisper. "But you still chose him over me."

"I didn't mean to—" Xander says, still without looking at me. "Just do what you have to do." He walks away, and I hear his door slam.

I lie on my bed for an hour staring at the ceiling. How could Xander not tell me his secret? What could be so bad, he couldn't even trust me with it? I clutch my cell phone in my hand. Robotically, I dial Freddy's number.

His familiar voice answers right before it was about to hit voicemail.

A small part of me wants to scream at him, call him out on all his lies, and throw every nasty word in the book at him. A bigger part of me just wants to hang up.

"Hey, it's Alice," I whisper.

I think it takes less than a minute to break up with him. It's the distance, I say. I'm overwhelmed with the women's league and figure skating and school. I'll miss him very much.

He grunts a: "Yeah, no worries. Makes sense."

"Bye, Freddy," I say.

"Wait, Alice," he says, his voice losing a bit of its confidence. "Did Xander say anything to you?"

I take a deep breath. I'm not an actor like Xander or Madison, but I need to pull this off. "No, I haven't talked to him since he got home. Why?"

"No reason. See ya around."

"Bye."

I bury my face in my hands and take a deep breath. My whole body feels numb. Maybe Xander says there's no secret, and maybe there isn't. But just in case, no matter how badly I want to chew Freddy out for what he did, I have to protect my brother.

I take a deep breath. Xander's right. I have to let Freddy and this secret go and just concentrate on what's important: the game.

Chapter Eight

HAYDEN

Bell's ratty car pulls up to the rink. Heh. I'm kind of surprised he showed. I thought for sure he was going to bail on this. It's been a couple of weeks since our road trip to Detroit, and since it seems like I won't be getting rid of this rookie anytime soon, it only makes sense to put him to work. He needs to learn how to hold his own in a fight, and eh, maybe I could use a few pointers on how to control my temper.

He gets out of the car, his hockey bag slung over his shoulder. He's swimming in an oversize sweatshirt and baggy jeans. A ball cap smushes down his shaggy hair.

"Okay," I say, "so what should we do first? Fighting or… y'know, working on my temper thing."

"Definitely the fighting thing," Bell says. "Because by the time that's done, I'm sure you'll have lots of anger you'll need to control."

We've got a few days off from playing, so I thought I'd take Bell down to the rink and teach him a thing or two about standing your ground while fighting. We've played a couple games since the one against the Ice Wolves, and I guess Coach Z thinks we make a good team, because he keeps playing us on the same line.

I guess I finally have to admit to myself that the kid's a good player, and he gets better every game. Soon, the other teams are going to notice, and he's going to become a target. He'd better at least learn how not to have some goon rip off his jersey.

I mean, I'm not gonna be responsible for him...but I can at least make sure he doesn't become an ice pancake.

We head out onto the ice, and Bell skates a couple laps. He's a natural, more comfortable in skates than sneakers.

"All right, let's get started." I skate over to him. "Gloves off. You're in a fight, aren't you?"

Bell nods, wearing that deer-in-the-headlights look I've become accustomed to. I chuckle and raise my hands, and he copies me. I reach over and grab his right arm. "So you want to try and hold back the other guy's punching arm. Stop him from going at you."

Bell reaches up and grabs my arm. He's so much shorter than I am, it's almost funny.

"You can also grab onto the other player's jersey," I say, twisting my hand in his hoodie. Bell pushes me away and skates backward.

I laugh. "Dude, I'm not going to actually fight you! Chill out!"

"Yeah, uh, I know that," he says, sticking his hands in his hoodie. He looks everywhere but at my face before skating back. "Okay, uh, yeah, whatever."

I raise my eyebrows and reach for his hoodie again— slowly this time. "Cool?"

Bell looks up at me, and his eyes are wide, questioning... as if he wants something from me but doesn't know how to ask. "Yeah," he says, his voice a high whisper. "Cool."

The way he's watching me—it weirds me out, but I don't back away. "All right," I say, "follow my lead."

An hour slips away from us as I go through all my moves—holding the other guy to keep balance, tearing helmets off, how to deke around a guy's fist. Just the basic stuff.

"How did you learn all this?" Bell wheezes, as we lean against the boards for a break.

"You just pick up tricks along the way." I shrug. "I'm always the guy getting into fights. When one of my teammates gets knocked down, I'm there to protect them. It's just my thing."

"Your thing?" He looks up at me, scrunching up his face. "Most guy's hockey thing is passing or shooting or speed… not being an elite goon. You're too good a player for that."

I look out to the ice. "I'm a better player than you, rookie."

"I believe this rookie is almost tied with you in points."

I throw my head back and laugh. "Because I'm always feeding you goals."

"Sure, Tremblay."

"I guess…I just really needed my own thing," I say, not sure he even cares. But there's something about the way he's looking at me that makes me think he does. "I was always the other Tremblay, the kid brother. Kevin already had the scoring record, the points, the trophies. He's been the captain of every goddamn team he's ever been on. I couldn't beat any of those records…so I needed something that he never did, something that was all mine."

Bell's eyes are trained on me. "And that thing is fighting?"

"I like the way the guys look to me. They know I have their back."

"I get that." Bell takes off his ball cap and runs a hand through his scraggly hair. "But…"

"What?" There's something he's holding back, because

he's scared I won't like it.

"It's just," he says, "I think it's more than that. Don't get mad, but from what I've seen, you seek it out. You look for fights."

"But if I can't fight, what kind of player am I?" I shake my head. "I'd just be...worthless."

Bell doesn't say anything. He just looks at me with that dumb, wide-eyed look on his face.

"S-sorry," I stammer, running a hand over my jaw. "I didn't mean to get all emotional on you and shit. Dude, you're worse than girl. Got me talking about feelings and shit."

. . .

ALICE

My heart hammers so loud, it almost drowns out my stupid panting. I can't stop staring at him. I'm pretty sure Hayden's never told anyone the things he's telling me. He looks almost helpless right now. His hair's tousled and stuck to his forehead with sweat, but I can still see the intensity in his dark eyes.

Hayden's not the only one experiencing something new by talking about feelings. There's nothing I hate more than having to explain myself. I've always figured that saying stuff out loud was useless, that if people want to fix something, they just have to go out and do it.

But listening to Hayden...it's like he's realizing this stuff about his brother for the first time...just by saying it. And even more surprising: I care, and I want him to tell me more.

But why?

"What kind of player do you want to be?" I ask.

He squints his eyes and looks up. "The year before my brother got drafted, he broke the record for most points in the junior league. The only record I broke last year was most fights in the season."

"Yeah," I say and cross my arms. "And how many games were you suspended for?"

"Five," he says, grinding his teeth.

"Can't break many records when you're not playing." I jokingly hit his arm, but he doesn't react. My hand lingers on his sleeve. Is this comforting or weird? All I know is, every instinct in my body is telling me to keep touching him.

He looks at me—really looks at me. And for a second, I wish he could see right through this whole Al thing. I wish I could just be a girl with a boy. A fantasy of pressing my lips to his, falling against his hard chest, clouds my thoughts.

But there's no way he's thinking the same thing, considering that I'm a boy.

"Um," Hayden says, "why is your hand on my arm?"

Oh shit.

I skate away from him.

"Anywaysss," I say, pretending to search for something in my pocket, even though we both know there's nothing there, "in case you didn't get what I was saying—stop being such a scaredy cat and actually play the game instead of hiding behind those fists of yours."

Hayden raises his eyebrows and looks at me like I'm some sort of mutant.

"Hayden?"

The bright lights of the arena sparkle in his dark eyes. "Okay, I think it's my turn."

"Right! Controlling your temper!" I bite the inside of my cheek. "So we've established that you fight because you're passionate about the game. Maybe we just have to channel that passion into a different area."

"What do you suggest?" He skates out to the ice. For someone so tall, he's awfully graceful.

I swallow in a dry throat. "How about...let's concentrate on making a playoff spot!"

He scoffs. "Obviously. But how do we do that?"

"More goals and more points," I say. "We're always on a line together. Maybe we can spend some extra time on the rink, work on some moves together..." I know Xander would not be happy if he knew I wanted to spend more time with the number one player on the Falcons, but hey, this is for the good of the team! And now that Hayden's been passing to me, we've been lighting up the rink almost every game.

Hayden stops at the net and leans against it. "Y'know, that's not the worst idea. But do you really think just the two of us can make some points happen?"

"Look," I say, skating toward him, "we're already good. This way we could be great!"

He narrows his eyes at me. "What are you smirking at?"

"My awesome plan." I smile.

"That hardly classifies as a plan." He laughs. "Play more hockey! Remind me not to include you when I'm figuring out how to survive a zombie apocalypse." He pushes me, and I glide backward.

"Come on!" I laugh. "It'll work and if it doesn't...we'll go back and think of something new."

"No, you'll be fired from planning ever again!" he says. His voice deepens, and I can tell he's serious. "But y'know, since it's your only plan...I guess I'll try it."

"Good."

"And Al," he says—and my world stops. He called me Al. Not Bell. Not rookie. Al. And for a moment, I close my eyes and can almost imagine that's my real name.

When I open my eyes, it gets worse. He gives me that narrow-eyed half-grin. The one that makes me think he has x-ray vision and is peering into my soul. "Thanks."

I swallow, remind myself to deepen my voice, then shrug. "No problem, man."

We leave the ice and I'm thinking I did a pretty good job

of holding it together as a dude—until I get into my car and see my reflection in the dashboard mirror.

A giant blush covers my entire face.

• • •

Hayden is on my mind the whole next day at school. It's so *annoying!* The last thing I should be worrying about is Hayden Tremblay. At least Madison is coming over this afternoon, so I'll have a distraction.

I can't remember the last time I've had a female friend, but Madison is just so gosh-darn *nice,* she made it impossible not to want to be around her. At the rink, she's a reassuring figure that I'm not so alone in this lie. And she's always hanging around our house, going over lines with Xander or wooing Mom with a flash of her gorgeous long hair.

As we walk home, she trills the whole time about how amazing Xander is at theater and dishes gossip on the Falcons' players. I'm surprised to hear there's no dirt on Hayden.

"He's so boring," she says. "He goes to the rink, and then goes home! Not like Sacachelli. Now he's got an exciting list of extracurriculars—"

Mom's silver van is parked in the driveway. I check my watch: just after 4:00 p.m.

"That's weird," I say to Madison as we walk up to my front door.

"What is?" She heaves her heavy pink backpack further over her shoulders.

"Mom's never home this early."

The moment my hand touches the doorknob, it's like a dark energy fills me. Sometimes I swear I'm psychic and can sense Mom's wrath the way a sorcerer senses magic. "Actually, maybe we should study at your house—"

"ALICE BELL!" The roar rattles the house even before

I open the door.

"Is it too late to run?" Madison squeaks.

The door flings open, and we're faced with my mother, red-faced and sweating. Smudged eyeliner runs down her face: a very uncommon occurrence.

"Afternoon, Mother Dearest," I say, avoiding eye contact. I snatch Madison's hand and drag her past Mom and into the living room, heading for the stairs. "We've got a big test coming up, so we have to study. All night. You probably won't see me for days—"

"Alice Magnolia Bell, don't you dare take another step." An evil smile forces it's way across Mom's tight face as she turns to Madison. "Madison, darling, how are you? You look wonderful. Would you excuse us for a moment?"

"Nice to see you, Rosaline! Of course, whatever you need," Madison says. She squeezes my shoulder and whispers, "Good luck!" before running up the stairs.

I'd breathe a sigh of relief that Madison won't witness the reaming of a century, except if I know Mom, she'll be loud enough for Madison to hear even upstairs in my room.

"What is *this*?" Mom snaps and holds out a piece of paper for me to examine.

"Uh," I mumble, looking away. I already know what's on it. "A note? For you."

A low growl rumbles in the back of Mom's throat that swings up into a falsetto as she reads the note aloud: "Mom, I can't go to Mexico for Christmas this year. I have hockey. From Al."

I give her a terse nod and a smile. "That's what it says, all right."

Mom squeezes the bridge of her nose. "Alice, what do you mean you can't come to Mexico? We go every single year. The owner, D'Angelo, is expecting you!"

"That's just it, Ma. We go every year. And this year, I have a hockey game." It's not a lie. If I go on our annual Christmas vacation to Mexico—which isn't really a Christmas vacation at all, but an excuse for Mom to drink and burn on the beach for a week while ignoring Xander and me—then I will miss a few games for the Falcons. I'm sure I could find a way to explain it to Coach Z, but I don't want to stop training. I worked so hard to be here.

And besides, I don't want to go. I've gone every single year for eleven years, and it's always the same. And especially now that Xander's decided to ignore me every waking minute of the day, there's no point. He'll probably love a Mexican vacation without me: no one will force him to go parasailing or ride up a rocky mountain on a donkey.

"Hockey?" Mom snarls. "That's all you ever think about! Hockey, hockey, hockey! It's just some silly recreational league! What about your family?"

"What about *your* family, Ma?" I snap back. "All you ever think about is yourself. Xander and I don't even like Mexico! It's too hot, the sand gets everywhere, and I can't sit by a pool for seven days without wanting to die of boredom. I'm not going this year!"

Mom's lip trembles, and I expect her to start yelling again. But she doesn't. Her eyes shine brightly. "Fine. If you hate it so much, you don't have to come."

"Mom," I say, stepping forward, but she grabs her coat.

"I need to go to the office," she says. "I'll cancel your plane ticket."

"Mom, can't you understand how important this is to me?"

"Yes, I understand. Whatever is best for Alice," Mom snivels and slams the door.

I stand there in silence for a minute, maybe longer. A strange feeling prickles at the back of my eyelids, and my throat is tight. Maybe it would feel good to collapse on the floor, sobbing and screaming about how it wasn't fair that Mom made me the bad guy when it's she who doesn't understand me.

I even try. I slam my eyes shut, trying to squeeze a few tears out. Maybe if they saw me cry, Xander and Mom wouldn't seem so distant.

But I can't. This is just how I am: hard and cold as the ice I skate on every day. And now I have to go upstairs and face Madison, which is the last thing I want to do.

It's not that I don't like her—it's just...I'm not good at having friends. I've never been good at it. It's just easier to deal with this stuff on my own.

I trudge up the steps to my bedroom. Madison waits on the bed, brow furrowed.

"Did you hear all that?" I say.

"Yes," she says and pats the bed. "Come on, sit down. Let's talk about it."

Slowly, I slump down beside her. "I'm sorry," I say. "First you find out I'm a crossdressing weirdo, and now you realize what a dysfunctional family we are!"

Madison smiles. "Don't worry. All families are dysfunctional."

I stare at her, with her perfect made-up face, and designer clothes, and that bright smile she always wears. "Not your family, though."

She laughs. "Trust me! My family is super dysfunctional."

A small smile creeps on my face. I was kind of nervous to bring Madison home to study, without Xander here to carry the conversation. But it's nice to be open with someone—God knows I can't tell Mom, Xander, or even Hayden everything.

"So you don't want to go on a family vacation with your fam?" Madison asks.

"We go every year! Can't we just have a normal Christmas for once? With snow and wrapped presents and stockings and

Santa? If I have to see D'Angelo in a fake white beard one more time…"

"Why didn't you just talk to your Mom about it?" Madison says, as if it were just that easy.

I stand up and pace away. I've never talked to anyone about this besides Xander, not even Freddy. "Our dad left around Christmas, so it's like, kind of a sore spot for Mom, I think."

"Oh," she says. "I'm sorry."

"It's cool. We were like five, so I don't really remember him. None of us have heard from him since, and that's fine with me." I peek a look back at Madison to see if she's getting weirded out by all my family drama, but she just stares intently, listening.

"That must be hard on your Mom."

Immediately, my stomach feels like it's twisting into a ball. I don't want to think about Dad or any of it. "Yeah, well it's hard on me, too. Mom checked out after that. She doesn't care about anything I want. She doesn't even try to understand me! What if I want a real Christmas, huh? Doesn't matter to her."

Madison flops down on the bed, her long hair pooling around her face. "Yeah, my *appa* is like that. It's med school for me, and that's that. Doesn't matter what I want to do. That's why I have to do all these extracurriculars on top of school, like volunteering for the Falcons. It's all to build that resume up."

"And theater?'

"No," she says, and her eyes shine. "I had to convince my dad that theater would look good on my resume. I didn't tell him that it wasn't my med school resume I was talking about."

I sit back down beside her. "What do you want to do?"

Her eyes flash with evil mirth. "I want to star in Korean

dramas!"

"What are those?"

She gives me the biggest smile I've ever seen and yanks her laptop out of her bag. "I'll show you!"

Our textbooks go untouched for the next three hours and my worries are forgotten as Madison and I binge-watch quirky show after show.

"I never thought subtitles could be so funny," I laugh as the credits roll of what has to be our fourth episode.

"I'll teach you Korean—it's even better. Then when I'm a big star in Korea, you won't have to miss me so much."

"You can't move to Korea! Then Xander and I would only have each other."

"Don't worry." Her face falls slightly. "Besides, it'll never happen. *Appa* says it's the doctor's life for me."

"That really sucks."

Madison looks at me and smirks. "It's okay. Your life is pretty much like a Korean drama, so it'll tide me over. All the cross-dressing and secrets! You just need one of those cute boys to fall in love with you, and then it would be perfect."

I raise my eyebrows and laugh. "Yeah, okay. Keep dreaming."

"Anyway," she says looking down, "if I didn't do all this extra stuff, I wouldn't have met you or Xander!"

A flash of warmth creeps over my skin. Maybe being alone is a little overrated after all.

Chapter Nine

ALICE

"I look like figure skating Barbie." I grimace as I hold the mirror up to my face. Madison has made me up with fake eyelashes and fifty pounds of makeup and put sparkles in my long brown hair extensions.

"Oh sweetheart, you look gorgeous!" Ma pops her head into the room.

I nod meekly. The first time I saw Ma after our fight about Mexico, she acted like nothing had happened. I had expected her to go on and on about what a wonderful time she and Xander were going to have, what kind of magical excursions she would do with the extra money from my plane ticket... but she just acted like it never happened. That's how I know I really hurt her.

And it's the same with Xander. We've both buried our fight deep down in the vault. Things definitely aren't the same—he pretty much ignores me whenever Madison's not around—but I'll just continue to navigate his moods as best

I can.

"Ready to leave in five?" She beams. The sad thing about my mom is that I can never tell if her smile is real or not.

I groan and try to flop down on the bed but Madison pulls me back up, yelling that I'm going to wrinkle my little white skate dress.

"Oh, and dumpling," Ma adds, "don't forget Channel 5 is going to be there! Hurry now, we can't be late! Xander, get dressed. You can't go in pajamas."

"Can't go, anyways, Mom." He smirks from my bed. He's taking full advantage of his broken leg to lounge anywhere he pleases.

Mom prances into the room, distastefully glancing over all my hockey and fantasy movie posters before settling her gaze on Madison. "Are you coming, darling?"

Madison nods and Mom's eyes light up. "Then of course you'll come, Xander! Keep the poor girl company."

Ahh, my mother's never-ending mission with Xander: to set him up with a girlfriend. So far it's proved a fruitless undertaking.

"Mother, I'm *ill*." Xander coughs meekly.

Mom rolls her eyes and sighs, toddling out to busy herself before she drags me to my own personal hell. As long as I'm there to twirl at the promotional event today for her Ice Ball, she doesn't care if Xander comes or not.

Which is a good thing, because if the real Alexander Bell—broken leg and all— showed up in front of the Falcons, things could get awkward fast.

When I agreed to do Ma's figure skating Ice Ball in the spring, I thought it was the only way I could stay on the ice. Now my two worlds are colliding, and I can only hope that Madison's disguise can hide Al from the Falcons. Because today, the Royal Chicago Figure Skating Co. is meeting up with the Chicago Falcons to promote their 3rd Annual

Charity Ice Ball. It's a huge event, and apparently this is their great idea to promote it.

And it might just ruin my entire life.

"Okay," Madison says, dabbing my cheeks with yet another layer of blush. "We've made you look unrecognizable from Al….but you're also going to have to act unrecognizable."

"What if I talk like this?" I say through a forced smile, raising my voice ten octaves.

Xander cringes. "Less demon My Little Pony and more Disney princess."

I huff. How did acting like a boy become easier than being a girl?

"Just be aware of the way you move," Madison says. "Sway your hips, don't clomp around like you usually do."

"I'll be on skates!"

"Still." She eyes me with concern through her thick curtain of midnight black hair. "You know the drill. For the first part, you'll be teaching the hockey boys a simple figure skating routine."

My stomach twists sickeningly. Any other time, I would pay to see the boys attempt a lunge or bunny hop. Now, the thought makes me want to throw up.

"And the second half," Madison said, eyeing Xander, "is where the boys teach the figure skaters some basic hockey moves."

"So what? That'll be easy." I shrug. Despite my nerves, I really wish I'd eaten something before Madison covered my lips in this bright sticky chemical.

"But that's it." Xander leans forward. "It shouldn't be easy. Not for Alice Bell, the figure skater. You'll blow the whole thing if you go out there and skate the same way Al does!"

"Oh…" I say, finally understanding what they mean. "I can suck at hockey for a night. I can do that."

"Can you?" Madison says, crossing her arms. "You're the most competitive person I've ever met."

My phone buzzes in my hand, and saves me from their utter lack of faith. Hayden's face flashes on it, and I have to will my heart to be still. I drift to the corner of my bedroom before answering.

"Hey Al," Hayden says, "I'm just about to head down to the rink. Want me to grab you on the way?"

Well, what do you know: my house isn't on the way to the rink. Dare I say we're becoming friends? My excitement will have to wait until I hang up the phone.

"Hey...uh, I'm not gonna make it..." Obviously Al can't be there at the same time as Alice Bell, figure skater. I'd much rather have Coach Z be pissy at me than endure my mother's fury for skipping out on this.

"Are you kidding me?" Hayden says. "You're going to make me suffer through figure skating alone?"

"COUGH COUGH COUGGGGGH!" I hack away, doing a much better sick impression than my so-called actor brother.

"Oh damn. That's nasty." Hayden laughs on the other end. "Rest up for the next game. See ya."

I hang up the phone, pretty pleased with myself. But when I turn around, Xander is giving me a look that's equal parts angry and terrified.

"Wha—"

"Who was that?" he says.

"Hayden, from the Falc—"

"Why are you smiling like that?"

I feel the muscles in my face fall immediately. I guess I had been smiling.

"Do you always smile like that when you talk to boys on the team?" Xander snaps. He sounds legitimately pissed. I feel my stomach drop and my veins go cold. "Alice, you're supposed to be *me* out there. Not you, okay? Everything you do affects my whole life."

My blood starts to simmer, boiling away the cold and nervousness. Xander's being such a dick! Here I am, helping him, and he's getting on me about one stupid phone call?

I walk to the door. "Come on, Madison. We should go."

Xander crosses his arms and looks out the window. I can tell he wants to storm away, but with his bum leg, it would take too long. I want to tell him he's being an asshole, but that would involve talking, which is not something I do, well, ever. I just want things to go back to normal, before I found out Xander was keeping some secret from me.

I grab my bag and huff out of the room. Madison lingers a moment, saying something too low for me to hear before scurrying after me.

I just have to get through one horrible night of figure skating, then tomorrow I can finally put all this anger where it belongs.

In the game.

• • •

I step onto the ice feeling completely naked and exposed. I need my pads, my jersey, my stick...not this glittery white dress that could potentially blind someone if they're caught in the wrong light. Although, I bet I'll look pretty sweet when I perform a backspin.

The arena glows with hot white light and bodies run around like frantic insects, setting up cameras and microphones. I watch their sneakered feet shuffle across the ice and bite the inside of my lip. I spot Ma standing with the two other figure skaters involved in the promotional event, Harmony and Liv.

They seem so natural in their tiny orange and blue

dresses, with their hair pulled back in tight buns, and their eyes bright and clear, not bloodshot red from too much mascara and eyelash glue.

I've never wanted a helmet so badly.

Just as I skate over, they burst into a fit of whispers and giggle. I look over my shoulder to see the Falcons filing onto the ice. An annoyed breath rushes out of my nostrils.

Girls.

The Falcons aren't wearing their full uniforms for this, just their jerseys and jeans. And what a bunch of losers! They look like they've all prepped to be camera-ready by styling their hair. I laugh a little to myself, imagining them scrambling to borrow Daniel Sacachelli's hair gel. God knows he has enough to spare. I swear that boy has fifty tubes in his locker.

Harmony lets out a particularly high-pitched giggle and grips my arm like a lifeline. "Oh my gawd. Number 9 is so dreamy, and he's staring RIGHT at me."

I shake her off. Number 9. Stupid, dumb, idiot Hayden. He's here for charity, not to ogle Harmony in her orange sparkly dress. I glare at him—but end up making eye contact instead. He's not staring at Harmony. He's staring at me.

I swallow and try to look away—but another part of me just *really* needs to look at him right now. His hair looks particularly wavy tonight, falling a little bit in his face. His jersey looks a tad big for him without all his pads on. He flashes a white grin.

I glare down at Harmony. "Number 9 is a total jerk."

Harmony doesn't seem to hear me; she's fixated on him. I huff and turn to the organizer, who's breaking us into groups. Lord, help me if I'm with Tremblay. *Anyone but Hayden, anyone but Hayden…*

• • •

I'm with Hayden. This is terrible. The worst. Out of everyone on the Falcons, I've definitely spent the most time with him. What if he recognizes me?

The organizers split the hockey players into even groups between Harmony, Liv, and me. We're supposed to teach them a simple routine, and then be judged by a panel. As little as I care about these expert judges (Ma and a few other ladies on the charity board), they've made this a competition and I hate to lose. Ever.

I breathe in through my nose and out through my mouth, trying to settle my unease. Between the cameras, hiding my identity, and Hayden skating over to me with that small smile, I've got choices about what to stress about.

My boys stand in an awkward huddle, waiting for me to instruct them. But I'm frozen, staring at Hayden who shifts from skate to skate. Suddenly, the lights seem unbearably bright and sweat pearls on the back of my neck. They're just staring at me, like children.

I skate back and forth in front of them for a couple moments, thinking about exactly what I'm going to say, and how I'm going to say it. On the other end of the rink, I already hear Harmony and Liv chirping on about pointed toes and graceful hand movements.

I can put it off no longer. "Hi guys! I'm Alice Bell! Today I'll be teaching you how to skate!" Okay, was that demon-pony or princess-like? Judging by their faces, I think I was verging on the side of demon.

"Okay, so you all know how to skate, but I'm going to show you...uh, how to figure skate." I skim over their faces to avoid eye contact. No one's yelling out, '*You're Al Bell!*' so I guess I'm okay.

Liv and Harmony's groups are already practicing. I really have to get going.

I break into a quick explanation of the moves and routine

we're going to do. When I finish, no one moves. I clap my hands. "Okay, so go!"

Half of them are looking at me with glazed eyes, and the other half stare at Harmony and Liv in their sparkling dresses. A small victorious piece of me is glad to say Hayden's in the former camp.

A part of me wants to get right up in their faces and remind them that I'm in a sparkly dress, too. But that would be weird, on so many levels. Regardless, my teaching method isn't working. This is my team and I know how they work.

I stare at them through my thick fake lashes and lower my voice ever so slightly: "Are you going to listen?" I bellow. "Right now, we're going to focus and learn to spin! Sacachelli is over there gliding flawlessly, and I know you'd all hate to be shown up by him!"

Their bodies snap to attention, and I get to work teaching them the routine. Surprisingly, they're better than I thought they'd be. Tyler Evans in the best, naturally gliding circles around the other boys. But I've got one rotten member of the group, one person who is standing in the back, one person who thinks he's too cool for all this. As much as I want to avoid Hayden as Alice, he's bringing down my whole team.

"Hey Hayden," I say, skating up, "how's your spiral coming?"

He looks over at me, smirking. "Ahh, the surly figure skater. Is this your revenge for having to share the ice with me?"

I cross my arms. I'd almost completely forgotten about that night. "You're too worried about falling forward. If you actually lift your back leg up, it'll counter balance. Here, let me show you."

I bend forward, sliding over the ice on one leg with my other leg straight out behind me. I turn back to him with a flourished twirl, just so he can see how pretty my skirt is when it spins.

He shakes his head but actually gives it a go. He still hardly brings his back leg up, but his back posture is admirable. He laughs as he loses his balance. "God, I wish your brother were here. That'd be hilarious to watch."

"Xander?" I say with a laugh. "He always liked figure skating better than me."

Hayden grins. "Al likes figure skating and yet he completely bailed on today! Do me a favor and kill him for me."

I give a meek smile and turn away. There I go again, saying things I shouldn't. Xander would kill me if he knew I told one of his future teammates what a figure skating buff he is.

Thankfully the TV crew saves me from my guilt. It's time for judging.

My team performs our routine for the judges and cameras, pulling a reasonable 7/10. Not terrible, considering Tyler and I carried the whole team. But Liv's team scores a 9, and Harmony and Sacachelli clean up with a full 10/10.

Now we switch and it's time for the boys to teach me hockey. I could totally redeem our miserable score in this round. I skate over to the sideboards and take a stick from the trainer. With dismay, I realize it's nearly a foot too short for me. Just because Harmon-o and Livvy are five-foot-nothing doesn't mean I should have to suffer along with them.

"AL-ICE," Madison says, somehow managing to turn my name into two syllables. She stands on the bench, dark eyes shooting daggers at me.

"What?"

"Don't even think about it."

I skate right up to her. "Come on."

"I saw the way you were looking at that score board. None of that matters. What matters is *Al*."

"Don't worry about it. I couldn't score anything with this." I hold up the cheap hockey stick they gave me, more closely resembling a twig than real sports equipment.

She narrows her eyes and I wink at her as I skate back to my teammates.

We start out of with a basic drill: weaving the puck between some orange cones on the ice. Child's play. Harmony and Liv barely make it through the first two cones.

"Looks like you've finally figured out how to hold a stick." Hayden skates up behind me.

"Huh?" Shoot, I really shouldn't know how to hold a stick. I fiddle with the twig in my hands. "Uh, my brother gave me some pointers earlier."

"Let's hope it helps. You're up."

Even with this useless stick, I'm able to keep the puck perfectly balanced on my blade. I maneuver through the first two cones with ease. I chance a glance up, to see Madison slowly shaking her head back and forth. With a sigh, I "lose control" of the puck after my third cone.

"Whoops," I say, shrugging my shoulders and go back to my team. We regroup and they give me some pointers, although I think some of their helpful stickhandling tips are just an excuse to get close against me. *Gross.* There's not much time to think. Minutes later, we're on to the next activity.

Task two: Shooting a puck from the blue line. I shoot and intentionally miss by a mile.

And I die a million deaths inside.

And a million more when somehow Harmony shoots, falling face first on the ice, but her puck makes it in the net.

Task three: Winning a faceoff. I know the boys are told to go easy on us, and when I'm face to face with Sacachelli's grinning mug, he leaves me the largest gap ever to take it. But I let it go. I let goddamn Sacachelli win a faceoff against me.

And I die another million deaths.

And a million more when Hayden lets Liv "win" her faceoff.

Task four: Two on two for a five minute "game". The only rule is the figure skater either has to assist the goal, or score it herself. I don't know how much more of this I can take.

As everyone gets organized, Hayden skates over to me. "Hey Alice, could I give you some advice?"

"No," I say automatically. Shit—that's Al's response. Alice is supposed to be a sweet hockey-naive figure skater. I shake my eight pounds of hair and put on my sweetest smile. "Uh, yeah sure."

"Okay." He smiles shyly and comes up behind me, lacing his arms over mine, the way the other guys did when they were trying to give me "advice." But this doesn't feel wrong the way it did with my other teammates. This feels...different. Breath catches in my throat. The murmurs of conversations become background noise to the soft rise and fall of his breath. His hands — so much bigger than mine — rest softly over my fingers. His chin grazes my jaw, scratchy with his ever so slight shadow.

"You're holding the stick with a death grip. Relax," he says. I force myself to remain utterly still, so as not to turn my face to his. "You won't drop it. I promise."

I loosen my grip. I guess I have been holding the stick really hard. But with him pressed up against me, I'm as far from relaxed as I've been all day. He straightens and grabs the stick from me. "You're way too tall for this stick. Gimmie a sec."

Hayden darts off the ice, into the locker room, returning moments later. "This is your brother's. It'll work better."

"Thanks," I say and snatch my stick from him. With it back in my hand, I feel whole again.

"You're really great at that figure skating stuff," Hayden says, not meeting my gaze. "My brother and I were in classes when we were really little. My parents thought it would help us manoeuvre in hockey. The home videos are pretty funny..." He trails off.

My breath catches in my throat. I live for moments like these, these moments when his barriers fall away, even for a moment. "My mom did the same thing with Xander and me. She didn't want me to go to hockey practice with him, but I convinced her the more I skated, the better figure skater I would be. Backfired for her though—" I catch myself. "For me. I hated hockey. Obviously."

He nudges me with his shoulder. "Who knows, maybe I can awaken your love of the game again."

I stare dumbly at him, and I wouldn't doubt that a trail of drool dribbles down my chin.

"Hey, number 9! Girl!" One of the camera guys yells at us, and we both turn. "Get up here, it's show time."

. . .

Hayden and I get into position on the ice, and I glare fiercely at our competition. Sacachelli wiggles his brick-shaped eyebrows, and Harmony flounces about, using her stick as a stripper-pole prop. Heat rises in me. They've got a total score of eleven so far, meaning they'll be the champions of this whole stupid publicity stunt. We have a whopping six points, meaning we'd have to score six goals in five minutes to win.

Even with the goal difference, it should be a cakewalk. Two on two with Hayden as my partner and my stick back? Easy. Except I promised Madison and Xander I would bomb the hockey stuff.

Harmony and I square off at centre ice for the faceoff. For the first time today, I feel like I'm where I belong. Sacachelli is my only real obstacle, and he's obviously distracted by Harmony's fancy dress. And when I look over at Hayden, my stomach twists at the thought of letting him down. Especially after he showed me how to hold a hockey stick. What would one goal hurt? Really?

Just so I don't embarrass my team.

I briefly catch Madison's gaze from the bench. She shakes her head more frantically now, so I avert my eyes.

Just one goal.

The whistle blows and I snatch the puck away from Harmony before she can blink.

I skate forward and get into position in front of the net. Hayden's already there, but I don't even bother to pass it. I slapshot it into the net. Their goalie's eyes go wide but I bat my pine-needle lashes and shrug. "Lucky shot!"

Next round, I pass to Hayden after deking around Harmony. It's not my fault that he can score from basically anywhere.

But we don't stop. Hayden and I score goal after goal. I can't help myself: it's like breathing. Nothing exists except for the puck, the net, and Hayden.

Suddenly, a sharp whistle breaks the air and I shoot my eyes to the whiteboard where Ma keeps score.

Uh oh.

We didn't get six goals.

We got nine.

Hayden throws his stick on the ice with a familiar holler and opens his arms wide toward me. I should skate away as fast as I can, but I fall against him, matching his own elated grin.

"How'd you get so good?" he says.

"Guess you made me fall in love with hockey again," I say with a forced laughed.

Hayden flashes that grin the TV cameras have been fixated on all afternoon. "Hockey must run in the family."

Hayden keeps his arm around my waist as the TV crew

comes over to interview us about the upcoming Ice Ball and the supposed fun we had today. But I can't concentrate on their questions, not with Hayden's hand resting so perfectly on the curve of my body. One by one, unwanted thoughts invade my head.

I've ruined it. There's no way Hayden didn't recognize the pass I gave him was the one he'd rehearsed not two days ago with Al. And what will Xander think when he sees the footage?

Hayden takes the reins for most of the interview, and thankfully Ma pulls me away so she can get some shots of the figure skaters. I don't miss that Hayden's gaze follows me as I skate away...

Freaking creepy.

Once the event ends, I head as fast as I can out of the arena. Mom's heading straight to the office, so I'm on my own, which is perfect because I need to be fast. If Hayden is going to call me out, I need to be prepared.

I throw on my black hoodie and sling my figure skating bag over my shoulder. The exit door is just within my reach when I hear a loud "Hey!" from behind me. I stop automatically and look back to see Daniel Sacachelli. He's changed and his black hair is slick and wet from the shower. He saunters toward me and, for some reason, I stay rooted to the floor. As if standing perfectly still will make him not see me.

He gets a little too close and smiles. "Allie, right?"

"Alice," I murmur, surprised at how quiet my voice has suddenly become.

"Alice," Daniel repeats in his thick Long Island accent. "Too bad I wasn't in your group—"

Daniel stops short as someone slings an arm around his shoulder. "Get your own figure skater. Alice was on my team."

At the mention of my name, my eyes dart up and I'm face

to face with Hayden. Like Daniel, he must have just come from the showers. His hair is wet, curling a bit around his face. He wears a beige top that clings tight to his broad chest.

"This guy bugging you, Alice?" Hayden says, his arm still around Daniel. Hayden smiles at me, and it's another one I can add to the Hayden Tremblay Looks I Can't Explain Folder. His mouth is half-forced into a twisted grimace, and one of his eyebrows is too high.

"I didn't know Al had a sister," Daniel says, leaning back as if to examine me. "I see why he doesn't bring you around now."

"Yeah," Hayden laughs. "Pretty sure the Falcons would be requesting figure skating lessons all the time."

I stare blankly at the two of them. Then with sick understanding I realize…they're hitting on me! Daniel and Hayden! Sacachelli and Tremblay! Number 77 and 9! Hitting on me, Al! Their teammate! Number 44!

Daniel's smile creeps up the side of his face and he pulls out his phone. "Say, if I did want some *private lessons,* how would I *book* those?"

Hayden looks over at him, shooting him a glare usually reserved for the Ice Wolves.

I heave out all the breath I can muster. "Disgusting!" I shout. "Both of you!"

I storm through the exit. My body trembles with anger. What did I expect, that Hayden would come up and say, "Hey Alice, good game out there! Whatta pass!" the way he does with Al? Who am I kidding? Hayden didn't notice a single thing today about how I played hockey. All he, and the entire rest of the team, noticed was a figure skater in a sparkling dress.

I throw myself in my car and look down at the ends of the dress peeking out from under my hoodie. I don't even know why I was worried anyone would recognize me out there. Not a single person saw a hockey player on that ice.

It's better pretending to be Xander. Hayden doesn't see me as some girl skating around. I'm his teammate. Just another person playing hockey. And I'd better keep it that way.

Chapter Ten

HAYDEN

I scoop up the puck and slide around the backside of the net. I keep my eyes fixed on the other team's player who comes right at me, and with my eyes locked on him, I pass the puck to the side. Two seconds later I hear the buzz.

Goal!

That heart-racing feeling of scoring a goal runs through my body. The team engulfs Al in a celebratory huddle, but I grab his jersey and pull him out of the crowd before he gets sucked into the sea of blue. He gives me a sheepish grin.

"I'll have to watch that goal on the highlights," I say.

"Yeah," he says, "because what kind of crazy player doesn't even look where he's passing?"

"I knew you'd be there." We skate to the bench and I slug him on the shoulder.

I hate to admit it, but this stupid plan of his is actually sort of working. It's been three weeks since we've been practicing, and in that time, we've racked up a lot of points. And it has another plus—I haven't gotten into a single fight. I see tons of opportunities where I could throw down, but all I can think now is that it's two minutes where I could be out playing with Al. It's like he's opened up this new thought pattern in my brain.

And that's why I can't do anything to jeopardize our new partnership...like asking him for his hot sister's number. As much as Alice drifts across my brain while I'm zoning out at school or through one of Kevin's many lectures, I have to put her and her little white tutu out of my mind. She's Al's sister, and can never be anything more.

• • •

After the game, the team is in high spirits. Another win and the long weekend is coming up for Thanksgiving... Life is good for the Falcons.

I shrug my bag over my shoulder and head out into the cold November air. Al pads beside me like usual. I've taken to picking him up and dropping him off after practice so we can talk about plays.

"Big thanksgiving dinner tonight?" Al looks up, smiling.

I exhale and watch my breath cloud in the air. "My Thanksgiving was in October."

"Right." Al laughs. "Weird Canadian."

"What about you?"

Al laughs as if I just said the funniest thing on Earth.

"What?" I say.

"My family doesn't do holidays. My mom's always way too busy organizing some event or another."

I stop and gape at him. "No holidays? Not even birthdays? Or Christmas?!"

He darts his eyes away. "I don't even think I own a stocking."

"You have got to be kidding me." I picture our old house at Christmas time. Dad would spend hours stringing lights across the roof porch, and Mom would hang garlands from every bannister. Now that my aunt and uncle own the house, I wonder if they decorate it the same.

"It's okay," Al says. "Can't miss what you don't know."

"Well, if you're free tonight, Eleanor's making ribs. I know it's not turkey and stuffing, but she's an amazing cook."

He stops. "Wait. Dinner at your house?"

"Yeah. Dinner. It's what normal people do when they're hungry."

He stops. "But dinner with…Kevin Tremblay?"

I throw my head back and groan. "You're not invited, anymore."

He runs to catch up with me, yattering on about Kevin. So far I've been able to avoid him fanboying over my big brother, but I guess I should have expected this. "Okay, fine. But be cool."

· · ·

It's a drive to our house, and I know my brother chose it because it's in suburbia. Eleanor doesn't like big cities; she's used to the small suburb right outside of Winnipeg that we all grew up in.

"I think Eleanor's the only person on the planet to see every single one of Kevin's hockey games. She's gone to the arena even when she's dying from a cold, and sits there in the rink bundled from head to toe in blankets. Her dad was our hockey coach back in Manitoba, so she'd always travel to games with us."

We pull down a side street with tall oak trees that cast shadows on the road in the glimmer of the street light. All the houses look the same but I pull up to a red house with a chicken on the mailbox.

"This place is beautiful," Al says.

Is it? To me, it looks fake. All the houses look the same. "This is what they always wanted," I say. "All Kevin and Eleanor would talk about was growing up and buying a house. Whenever we drove through neighbourhoods like this, they'd point out the window and say which houses they liked."

"And you didn't?" Al glances sideways at me.

"Me?" I laugh. "I just wanted to get to the game."

"Of course," he says. "Driving to games always seems like the longest ride ever. I just want to get out there and play."

I jump out of the car, but Al lingers.

"I wish I'd worn something nicer," he mutters.

"It doesn't matter."

"But he's the captain of—"

"Right now," I say, "he's my brother. There's a difference."

Eleanor opens the door before we're even halfway up the driveway. Her big blue eyes are visible even in the twilight, and she's curled her blond hair. I texted her I was bringing a friend, so I guess I should have expected this: she's a born entertainer.

"Hello! Hello, hello, hello!" A huge smile beams on her face. She wears an apron embroidered with the logo of Kevin's hockey team.

We enter the house and she gives Al the tour. I don't spend a lot of time up here, besides grabbing food; it's always so spotless, like something pulled out of a home and garden magazine. Everything has a place.

All I can think is that it's everything our childhood home wasn't. Our house was a mess all the time. Mom never framed photos—they were always just stuck on the fridge. Sure, the house was chaos, but when you have two boys who only care about hockey, that's the way things are.

We sit down to dinner and I don't feel the tension I usually do when I'm forced to endure a meal with the Mister and Missus. For some reason, I feel so much more comfortable with Al here. It's almost like being on the ice: when I have my skates on, I know exactly who I am.

Al asks Kevin a million questions about the NHL throughout dinner, but I can tell he's trying to contain himself. Of course Mr. Captain eats it up—he never tires of talking about himself.

"Hayden," Eleanor says, and she does that thing where she holds my gaze to make sure I'm listening before she starts to talk. "Have you decided if you're coming?"

Kevin sighs. "Why do you even bother?" She's been asking me every day for the last month, and now even Kevin's grown tired of it. At least we're on the same page.

"Because one of these times," she says, "he's going to say yes."

I hide my satisfaction as I eat a spoonful of potatoes. Eleanor doesn't know how wrong she is.

"Go where?" Al bumps my shoulder and looks at me. I think it's the first time he's cast his gaze away from Kevin or his food all night.

"Back to Winnipeg for Christmas," Kevin says. "He didn't come last year."

"Why would I want to go to snowy old Winnipeg," I say, "when I can stay in snowy old Chicago?" I take a drink. I doubt Al wants to hear the sob story of the Tremblay brothers.

"I'll be here to keep you company," Al says.

"I thought for sure you'd head home," I say. "Detroit isn't far."

"The fam's going to Mexico," he says. "Mom didn't like it, but I insisted. I would have missed a game if I went, so I'm just gonna stay by myself."

"I'm sure the team wouldn't mind if you miss a couple games," Eleanor says.

Al's eyes go wide and he recoils as if she just suggested he give up breathing. "Are you kidding? This is playoff crunch time! Why the hell would I waste seven days eating crap and lying on a beach when I could be scoring points for the Falcons?"

I smile. I never thought I'd meet anyone who loves hockey as much as me. "Pizza and beer for Christmas?"

"Perfect." Al smiles.

. . .

ALICE

"Where are you going?" I say, as Hayden peels off the main road.

"A little detour." He flashes a small smirk.

I don't reply, just stare out the window. We've turned onto a gravel road, and the Jeep bounces beneath me. Dark trees watch us pass by like staring sentinels and the night seems to creep through the windows.

"You're not taking me out here to murder me, are you?"

Hayden raises a thick brow. "Don't be such a girl."

I give an awkward cough-laugh. "Just kidding," I say, my voice automatically deepening an octave and I spread my legs wider. "But hey, then you'd have no competition for number one player on the team."

He snorts. "Not really worried about that, Al." The Jeep rounds a corner and slowly comes to a stop. "Do you know why it's so cold tonight?"

Because it's winter in Chicago? But he seems onto something, so I keep my comment to myself.

"There's no clouds out tonight to keep the heat in. So it's clear." Hayden smiles, and it shoots right through me like an arrow. "Which makes it the perfect night for stargazing."

My whole body freezes and I'm sucked into that smile.

It's dark in the car, but I can picture the way his brown curls fall across his eyes, the slight raise of his eyebrows.

No one should be allowed to have a smile like that. Period.

"Come on," he says, and jumps out of the Jeep.

We could have landed on Mars and I would have followed him out. I'm used to being breathless by now.

We're in the middle of the goddamn woods, and I can barely see a foot in front of me. I really wish I hadn't made that joke about the whole murder thing, because now it feels like a distinct possibility.

"Come here, stupid," Hayden says, and I follow his voice to the front of the Jeep. He lies on the hood, arms behind his head. I've seen him lie like that countless times on one of the benches in the locker rooms, but he's usually shirtless. Yet here, he makes it look just as good in his fur-lined parka.

I jump on the hood beside him. "Whoa."

I've never seen so many stars. Spattered across the sky like chipped ice, my eyes get lost in their maze. Breath catches in my throat and I want to tell him it's the most beautiful thing I've ever seen. But that sounds sappy...lame...girly.

"This is cool, man," I manage to say, but it sounds forced and awkward. He doesn't reply. I grind my teeth, knowing I shouldn't add anything, but the words force out of my throat: "Why are you wasting this view on me? Seems like a perfect date spot."

"I've never taken a girl here," he says, then quickly: "I mean, I don't know. It's, like, my spot. A good place to think. I thought...I thought you'd get it, or something..." He trails off.

I do get it. I want to tell him it's beautiful, and when I look up into the sky, it's like I'm lost in all the millions of possibilities of the world. But when I look at him, I'm not lost anymore.

"I used to go to the roof of our local arena," I say. "When my br—err, sister, was in practice. I'd wait up there for her and just think."

"About what?" He turns, and I see the breath leave his lips.

"Everything," I say. "And absolutely nothing."

"I know what you mean." He closes his eyes. "You know what this view reminds me of? My dad used to build an ice rink in our backyard every winter. He'd stand out there for hours in the freezing cold with the hose. But I think Kevin and I spent more time out there than inside. We'd stay on the ice until the sun went down and then we'd beg Mom to turn the porch light on, even though it didn't help. Dad would come out to get us, but we'd rope him into playing..." He pauses, never taking his eyes off the stars. When he starts to talk again, his voice is deep and coarse. "And then Mom would come out and she'd have hot chocolate in everyone's thermos. We each had a different color. Mine was red. Kevin's was blue, Dad's was green, and Mom's was yellow. We'd lie on the snow beside the rink and look up at the stars. Just the four of us."

I have to look away from Hayden and keep my mouth shut because if I open it, I don't know what will come out. Because I know how this story ends. Even with Hayden never telling me, Kevin's famous enough to have his life story splattered all over the Internet.

I swallow but my throat is dry. All the hockey magazines and bloggers love to tell the underdog story of Kevin Tremblay, who got drafted to an NHL team right after his parents were killed in a terrible car accident. But here are the true broken pieces, laid out for me to see.

We sit in silence for a while until Hayden laughs. "The stars here are shit compared to Winnipeg though."

I clear my throat and laugh with him. "Blame all the

lights from the hockey arena."

He lets out a small breath, then says, "Hey, Al…"

"Yeah?"

He leans on one arm and looks over at me. "If I went back home, would you want to come?"

I suck in a breath. Hayden wants me to come back home with him? To the place where he hasn't been in over a year?

But not me. He wants Al.

"We won't miss any games! I promise."

I sit up a bit too and give him a small smile. "Sure, that'd be cool. I've never been to Winnipeg."

Hayden lies back down on the Jeep. "You'll see, the stars there are way better."

Chapter Eleven

ALICE

"HOLY F—" My expletive gets carried away on the wind as we step outside. "What frozen planet have you taken me to?" I try to scream at Hayden, but he just rolls his eyes at me.

"Are you joking?" he says. "This is T-shirt weather!"

I pull my beanie further over my ears and try to bury my face in my jacket. I thought I would be prepared for winter in Winnipeg after growing up near Detroit and living in Chicago, but this isn't winter. This is icy hell!

The wind whips Eleanor's scarf around her head as we quickly hurry to the rental car. "Don't worry, Al!" she says, her voice musical. "Your whole body will be numb soon enough and then you won't notice a thing!"

Despite the weather, a grin emerges on my face. I have four days in Winnipeg with Hayden for our holiday break. It's definitely better than spending it alone in Chicago while Mom and Xander frolic in Mexico.

Of course, Xander isn't happy. He gets on my case just

for seeing movies after practice with Hayden. Now that I'm spending four straight days with him…it's an understatement to say Xander is freaking out.

Inside, I'm freaking out, too. I'm pretty sure I've mastered being a boy on the ice, but it's hard enough keeping my voice deep and my shoulders broad whenever games end. And now, with my heart going into overdrive every time Hayden looks at me, how am I supposed to keep this up?

I look at Hayden. He was in good spirits when we boarded the plane; we passed the time watching bad Christmas movies and ordering junk food from the flight attendant. But now, he sits in the rental car, his shoulders slumped, gaze fixed out the window. Silent.

I want to lean into him, take his hand in mine, tell him it will be okay. But all I can do is stare straight ahead, and listen to Kevin ramble on about every single member of their large family.

Outside, there's only white. White plains, a white sky; even the air seems white. Kevin's voice is deep but soft, and my eyes grow heavy.

When I wake up, the sun has set and streetlights dust the snow with golden halos.

"We're 90% of the way there," Kevin says.

Hayden no longer looks out the window. He stares straight ahead, his fists taut.

Ten minutes later, we pull up to a house covered in multi-colored Christmas lights.

"It looks like we walked into one of those movies we watched on the plane," I joke, nudging Hayden's elbow. He doesn't respond.

Kevin shuts off the car and a stream of sweater-wearing Canadians exit the house. Kevin and Eleanor jump out, embracing them with huge hugs. Hayden slowly gets out of the car, and grabs the luggage from the back.

I follow him, watching my feet sink into the sloshy snow all the way up the driveway. "Y-you all right?"

He nods, looking up at the house. "Yeah...it's just... weird."

Hayden told me that after his parents died, his aunt and uncle bought the place and moved in. Everyone said it was best that the house remained with the family. My throat tightens as I look at Hayden's face, pale and tense. How strange it must be to go home, but have it not be your home at all.

We lug everything into the house. It's warm inside; not a perfectly set temperature kind-of warm, but a stuffy-with-people sort. His uncle greets us right away, and thankfully takes our hats and coats.

Then he leads us through the house. The whole thing is made of wood, with big log walls, and soft warm lights. With all the Christmas decorations, it gives off a Santa's-workshop kind-of vibe. We head into the living room, and in the corner is the biggest Christmas tree I've ever seen. There's a mishmash of ornaments, from homemade to silly Santas playing hockey. Eagerly, I breathe in that real-tree scent. A huge fire crackles in the fireplace, which is surrounded by people.

They all jump up and start talking at once, running over to Kevin, Eleanor, and Hayden. I meet my teammate's aunt and uncle, their two girls, a bunch of cousins, Eleanor's family, some old guy named Uncle Eldy (who isn't even a real uncle), an old hockey coach, a pastor, and more kids under two than I can count.

I look around for Hayden, but he's nowhere to be seen. Then I catch a glimpse of him heading up the stairs.

"Hayden sweetie!" his aunt Ginger calls. "You're in the last room to the right! There's some boxes to sort through up there, if you like."

Hayden doesn't respond. He turns robotically and storms

up the stairs.

Why would Hayden run away from this? This is *amazing*. I was too young to care that Mom stopped doing holidays once Dad left. Xander and I would just hang out, make food, give stupid presents. I didn't realize what I was missing.

But since Hayden has decided to turn into an emo teenager, I guess it's up to me to drag our bags up the eight million stairs to the room.

My lungs feel like they're going to collapse by the time I make it. Here I thought I'd get a little holiday break from working out. When I finally get to the last room on the right, I tap lightly on the door, and creep inside.

Hayden sits on the bed. There's a big cardboard box in front of him, with his name scrawled on top.

"Hey," I say lightly, and walk into the room.

I notice he's holding a pair of skates in his hands. I wonder if I've interrupted some personal reflective moment. I'm not good with that sort of stuff. I take a few steps back. "I'll come back later."

He looks up at me. "Huh? No, it's okay. I was just looking through this junk."

Shit. I reluctantly sit beside him. The skates in his hands look old and worn, and very small.

"I have no idea why they kept these," he murmurs and chucks them to the side. He flops down on the bed, sighing.

"Did this used to be your room?" I ask.

He shakes his head. "No, I think the girls use my old room now. This was my Mom's storage room. It started out as a place for her scrapbooking, but we kind of took it over… filled it with hockey gear, jerseys, trophies."

I smile and look around. It's bare in here now. "Yeah, our home was pretty cluttered too. Hockey takes up a lot of space."

"Tell me about it." He sighs and turns his head slightly

to me. A brown curl falls in front of his face, and I have to resist the urge to push it back. "I never thought I'd come back here."

"How long has it been?" I say.

He swallows and then sits up, arms falling over his legs. "Kevin was officially drafted by the NHL one week after they died." His voice hitches. "He took care of everything. I remember him asking if I wanted to stay here, to live with Doug and Ginger until I finished high school. But I didn't. Our family had always been close—just the four of us. I knew he wanted me to come with him, just as much as I didn't want to be here. He figured it all out, all by himself. Switched my schools, switched my team. The minute the funeral was over, we boarded a plane to Chicago—and the only thing I could think when I stepped off that plane was that I never wanted to come back here again."

He looks so broken, so fragile. I want to take his hand, let him know I'm here for him. But I can't. I put a hand on his shoulder. I don't have any words for him, but I think this will do for now.

Hayden leans down toward me. Here, in this tiny room, he looks so much smaller than he does on the ice.

A small smile flickers on his lips. "Thanks for doing this with me, Al," he says. "I'm real glad you're here."

"Me too." Even though everything I do is a lie, this is not. I am glad to be here.

· · ·

HAYDEN

"This is definitely not what I was expecting," Al mutters as we walk into the dining room.

"And what were you expecting?" I say.

"Moose-on-a-spit, fried beaver, everything drizzled in

maple syrup."

"Sorry to disappoint." I nudge his arm and carve out a spot around the huge table. It's hard to hear over the ruckus as my family laughs and shares stories. Chinese food cartons are littered all over the table. "I hope everyone's got their food, because Al is going to eat everything in front of him."

Everyone bursts out laughing, and Al's cheeks turn bright red. He blows a strand of hair out of his face and rolls his eyes.

"Hurry up and eat!" Aunt Ginger says, clearing away some of the empty cartons. "It's almost stocking time!"

A heavy weight sits on my chest. This is why I didn't want to come. Maybe Kevin thought going through all of this would help me find peace, but it doesn't. It just means I have to force a smile on my face and bury my thoughts farther away.

Al helps Ginger clean up. He's all smiles, and even carries the giant, dusty box of stockings up from the basement, straining under its weight. A smile flashes on my face.

My family takes turns picking their stockings out one by one. This is a new tradition. Before, four stockings hung on our fireplace, but since Mom and Dad died, and Ginger, Doug, and their kids moved in, Christmas has become an entire family affair. Or so I've been told.

Al bursts out laughing and I walk over. He holds my stocking.

"What?" I say.

"It's *plaid*," he says between laughs. "And has a moose on it!"

I snatch it from him and shove him in the arm. "Shut up."

His eyes crinkle with mirth and I catch myself smiling again. "Wait here," I say.

When I come back, I toss him a balled up piece of fabric. "One left."

Slowly, he holds it up: a plain red stocking. His name is

sewn across the fluffy white top.

His fingers trace the lining of his name. "A stocking? For me?"

I throw an arm behind my head and look away. "Yeah, well, I didn't want you to feel left out."

"You got this for me..." Al whispers, and his voice is quiet and soft.

"You gotta hang it yourself though, slacker," I say, handing him the hammer.

He snatches it eagerly. As he gives the nail one last hit, he turns to me, eyes shining. "Thanks, Hayden."

Usually I would tell him it was nothing, that it's just some stupid stocking and he shouldn't be such a sap. Instead, I say, "It's the least I could do."

"Announcement!" Eleanor's clear voice rings through the living room like a knife on a wine glass. Everyone turns to her. Kevin beams up from his armchair.

"I have an early Christmas present," she says, "for Kevin." She hands him a small wrapped gift.

He narrows his eyebrows and smiles. "What's this?" Carefully, he pulls off the wrapping paper.

Tears shine in his eyes and he covers his mouth. In an instant, he leaps from the chair and wraps Eleanor in his arms. She starts crying, too, her smile lighting up the whole room.

Then Kevin snatches up the present and holds it up for everyone to see. A small white stocking, with writing at the top that says, *Baby*.

"I'm going to be a dad!" he shouts.

The entire family erupts, looking just like the Falcons bench after we score a goal. They surround Kevin and Eleanor, swallowing them in hugs and shouting about champagne.

Al claps me on the shoulder. "Congrats, Uncle Hayden!"

Outside, my face holds a huge smile, and I can feel

myself joining in the happiness with my family, walking over to Kevin, hugging him and Eleanor, laughing about buying baby skates.

Inside, I feel nothing.

Chapter Twelve

ALICE

The ground is hard. And cold. Very cold.

Damn, Canada.

I roll over and pull the blankets up around my shoulder. When I offered to take the air mattress, Hayden didn't even put up a fight. I'm super regretting that now, figuring it's deflated to a very uncomfortable sheet. I bet he would have let me have the bed if he knew I was a girl. I wonder if we'd share the bed if he knew I was a girl...

I open my eyes to stop myself from going there. I have to stop thinking about Hayden like that. He's my friend. My teammate.

I sit up and look at the bed. Hayden's not there.

Where is he? I stand up and touch the sheets. They're cold. He's been gone for a while, then.

I peer around the dark room, not sure what I'm expecting to find. A glimpse of red catches my eye out the window. I rub away the frost and squint to see him, sitting outside in a snowbank, wearing his bright red hat.

What a crazy person, sitting outside in the cold on Christmas Eve! Well, at least the bed is up for grabs...when he comes back, he can sleep on the cold hard floor. But instead of cozying up under the covers, I find myself creeping downstairs, pulling on my hats, boots, and jacket and heading outside.

Obviously something is wrong. No sane person would be outside in this frozen wasteland. What if he wants to talk? That terrifies me. Yet still, I trudge across the snow to see him.

My stomach twists into a knot as I get close enough to see the clouds of breath gusting in front of his face. I stand behind him, afraid to break through the silence and moonlight. I see what Hayden stares at now. A makeshift ice rink, dusted with a thin layer of snow.

Is this like the one his dad used to make every year? The one his whole family would play on, and then sit and drink hot chocolate by every night?

"Hayden," I whisper.

He doesn't move, not for a very long time, then his head bows lower.

I kneel beside him. Tears streak down his face, and his teeth are gritted. "It's just not fair."

I don't know what to say. I've never been good at this stuff. And there's definitely nothing I can say that will make this hurt any less. But I settle down in the snow beside him. At least I can show him I'm not going anywhere.

Hayden reaches up and pulls his hat further over his eyes. A gasp tears from his throat. "I- I just...it's not fair. They should be here!" He tosses his hat onto the rink, where it lies like a dead beacon on the ice. "Kevin's having a baby! A baby! Mom...Mom would have loved that. She'd have been such a good grandma. Only she'll never get to see that baby.

She'll never get to see Kevin get married...or...or—" The strangled cry releases from his throat and he burrows his face in his gloves, gritting his fingers as if he could rip the feelings from his body.

"It's okay to be sad," I say lamely.

He looks up, head tilted back. "I can't even remember how I felt when it happened. Kevin told me. I cried, I think. I don't remember what I thought. Only that it felt like I was asleep. Like there was fog in my head and all I kept thinking was, 'This isn't real. I'm going to wake up soon. This isn't real.'"

I bite the inside of my lip. I know I shouldn't, but I reach out and put a hand on his shoulder. He doesn't pull away.

"I can't look at pictures of before," Hayden continues. "Kevin does all the time. He hangs them all over the house. Pictures of me and him and Mom and Dad out on the rink, in the kitchen, driving through town. Why does he do that? How can he stand to remember what it felt like?" Fresh tears stream down his face. "I just can't do it."

"Maybe," I say, "your heart hurt so much that day, it didn't want to feel again. Anything at all. Sometimes it's easier to feel nothing."

He gives a half-hearted laugh and wipes his nose. "Well, I think I'm feeling something now, Al," he says, "and I don't like it."

I drop my hand. "Should we, uh, go back inside?"

He stares at the rink. "Nah, not yet."

"Want something warm to drink?" I don't know about him, but I'm turning into an Alicicle out here.

He nods. "Sure. I'm gonna stay out here."

I get up and scurry toward the house. My heart hurts, seeing him sit there on the snow. He looks ten years old from here.

A wave of relief and warmth washes over me as I enter the

kitchen. Even with so much sadness, this place feels peaceful.

I turn on the light and dig through the cupboards as quietly as possible. There has to be mugs and hot chocolate somewhere. Isn't that part of the Canadian Starter Kit, along with a jug of maple syrup and a plaid saddle for your polar bear?

Just when I'm on my hands and knees, resorting to digging through the pots and pans for the hot chocolate powder, a voice floats through the kitchen: "Looking for this?"

I turn around, whacking my head on the roof of the cupboard. "Ouch!"

"Easy now!" Strong arms grab me and lift me to my feet. I look up at Kevin's smiling face, framed by his bushy beard.

My stomach drops. "Shoot, did I wake you?" I rub my sore head and avoid eye contact.

"I've been up for a while." Kevin turns on the kettle and taps a small jar beside it. "Hot chocolate is in here. Ginger makes her own powder."

"Ah," I say. An awkward silence fills the room as I wait for the water to boil. What is Kevin doing here? I'm still wearing my big winter jacket, so I don't have to worry about my binding coming loose.

"You know," Kevin says, and a wash of relief floods over me at the filled silence, "I don't think I thanked you for coming here."

"Thanked me?" I snort. "You paid for my ticket here. This is so much better than spending Christmas alone in Chicago."

"Y-you're a good friend to Hayden," Kevin says, and his eyes look past me, out the window. "And we both know he isn't the easiest person to get to know."

"Tell me about it," I grunt, then catch myself. My eyes follow Kevin's, to where Hayden sits in the moonlight. "Even so...he's my best friend."

A smile pricks on Kevin's lips, but he says nothing.

More silence.

Ugh, I'm terrible at this.

The whistle of the kettle rings through the air and I jump to take it off the heat.

"Coming here isn't easy for him," Kevin says. "I know that. But this"—he gestures to the kitchen and out the window—"is more than just a childhood home."

The heat of the kettle warms my hands, but I can't take my eyes off Kevin. He stands, hands on the edge of the sink, staring out into the snow.

"We dreamt here. Every wish, desire, every ounce of passion...it was cultivated in this home because of them. Because of our mother and father. And now I'm afraid without them"—he shakes his head—"Hayden's too sad to dream again."

I take an awkward step toward Kevin, still holding the boiling kettle. "Dreams are never really lost. Maybe coming back will give him the courage he needs to find them again."

Kevin flicks a small all-too familiar smile. "I hope that's so. I tried my best, you know, to fill Mom and Dad's void. To be a parent to him." A flash of pain crosses his face. "Maybe I forgot how to be a brother."

I put the kettle down and gingerly touch Kevin's arm. "Hey, Kevin," I say, then quickly cough and deepen my voice, "you did a great job. Hayden, well, maybe he doesn't show it, but he looks up to you." A blush rises to my cheeks. "And he's just...well, he's just the best guy I know."

Kevin raises an eyebrow and smirks.

Quickly, I jump to the cupboards. "Err, I'll grab some mugs for this hot chocolate!"

"I've got an idea." Kevin darts from the room for a moment, flying through the house with the speed and grace only a center would have.

When he returns, he's grinning from ear-to-ear like a little kid. In his hands, he carries two flaked, dull-colored thermoses.

"From your childhood." I smile.

He pours the water and stirs in the hot chocolate powder. He hands me a mug and then picks up the two thermoses. "I think this is my play, Al. Why don't you get some rest?"

Taking orders from Kevin Tremblay. This is like a dream come true. "Good night, Kevin."

I head back up the stairs and creep into the bedroom. I can't help but take a peek outside: Kevin walks over to Hayden and hands him his thermos. He puts an arm around his little brother.

I can't see from here, but I imagine they're smiling.

I steal an extra blanket from Hayden's bed and lie back down on the deflated air mattress. A strange sensation fills me. Right here, on this hard floor, in this cold room in Manitoba…it's exactly where I'm supposed to be.

• • •

HAYDEN

The stockings are opened, breakfast has been eaten, and we all wade through a flood of wrapping paper to enter the living room. The kids are passed out on the couch, and everyone meanders around, sipping coffee.

I didn't think it was possible, but being here…it's okay. I guess I thought coming home without Mom and Dad would make the pain worse. The emptiness is still there, but there's something with it, too. Being here, remembering all our happy memories…it feels like I'm honoring them. I'm glad my uncle has this house and his family gets to enjoy it. It really was the best place to grow up. This is what Mom and Dad would have wanted.

I look to Kevin. His arm wraps around Eleanor. This time next year, they'll have a baby. Someone new to love and care for.

I'll be an uncle. Holy shit.

I shake my head and catch sight of Al on the couch. He rests his face in his hands and stares out the window. He was so excited this morning when he saw "Santa" had filled his stocking, too. It was just junk and chocolate, but by his grin, you woulda thought he'd won the Stanley Cup.

I plop down on the couch beside him. "Whatcha looking at?"

He gives me a sideways glance, running a hand through his wayward hair. "The ice rink."

I follow his gaze. In the morning light, the rink doesn't fill me with the same sadness it did last night. "I guess it looks nice."

Al gives me that look of his.

"What?"

"Did you bring your skates?"

I raise my eyebrow. "Why would I bring my skates to Winnipeg?"

A smile breaks out across his face. "You totally did! So did I!"

"Okay, yeah." I shift uncomfortably. "Just in case we wanted to go to the local rink! Trust me, you don't wanna skate on that uneven, bumpy, backyard thing. Coach Z would skin us both if we hurt ourselves on that death trap!"

Al leaps to his feet. "Is the great Hayden Tremblay afraid I'll embarrass him in front of his family?"

I tighten my jaw. "Yeah right, Bell. You're just obsessed. Can you not go two days without skating?"

"Nope," Al says, and grabs my arm. "And neither can you."

I feign a sigh, but a smile works itself across my face. "I

hate it when you're right."

• • •

ALICE

It's only nine p.m., but I'm exhausted. The day was so full — full of gifts, food, love. I sit on the couch surrounded by all of Hayden's family, as a Christmas movie plays on TV. Most of the kids are in bed. Most of the adults look ready to pass out too, bellies full of turkey and Baileys.

I'll have lots of wonderful memories from the last few days, but watching Hayden step out on that ice rink has to top my list. He was a little kid, laughing and mouthing Kevin off when he came out to join us. With the whole deception-thing, it can be hard to remember that hockey is *fun*. Nothing like being out on a homemade ice rink with two brothers to remind me of that.

After hockey, I spent a good hour on the phone with Mom, who seems to have mostly forgiven me for not coming to Mexico. It sounded like they were having a fun holiday, but Xander didn't get on the phone once. Mom says he got a huge sunburn and isn't feeling well.

A hot flash of guilt washes over me. This is the first Christmas I've been away from Xander. Maybe we never had a real Christmas, but we were always together. We'd sit in the same hotel bed, side by side, and shut the blinds, blocking out the beaming Mexican sun so we could pretend it was snowing out. We'd watch Christmas movies all day, except for breaks to run down to the buffet and gorge ourselves. I wonder if he did any of that today.

I suddenly feel hot, and walk to the kitchen for a glass of water. These thoughts are stupid. I shouldn't be feeling guilty — I'm doing this for Xander!

Someone comes in the kitchen behind me. I spin around

to see Hayden. He's wearing the Christmas pajamas his aunt bought him: a white long-sleeve shirt and plaid flannel pants. It's about two sizes too small, so the shirt stretches tight across his chest and the pants only go down to his ankles. His hair is mussed, brown wavy curls falling everywhere, and his cheeks are flushed from sitting so close to the fire. I can't help but let out a little breath as I look at him.

I always wonder what version of Hayden is my favorite. Maybe the hockey player in his blue jersey, confidence radiating from him like heat from the sun. Locker room Hayden is also a winner, and not just 'cause he's usually shirtless (which is a total bonus) but because of his intensity, how he can bring a team together or pick us up when we're at our lowest. And then there's also Hayden outside the game, when we play video games and go to movies, and he wears his jeans and funny hats and stupid plaid shirts.

I savor him. I think pajamas Hayden might be my favorite yet.

"Hey," I say, smiling, "what's up?"

"It's super hot in there. Wanna get some fresh air?"

I follow him out of the kitchen into the foyer, where we throw on our jackets and boots and head out into the snow. The cool air feels good against my flushed face. It's so clear: stars stretching across the sky as far as the eye can see. Now I totally get what Clement C. Moore was trying to say about the moon on the breast of the new fallen snow. There's so much *light* out here. "You're right," I say. "The stars are better in Winnipeg."

"Told you."

I look back to the house. His family crowds on the couch through the orange glow of the window. "They're really in love, aren't they?" I say in a low voice.

"Huh?" Hayden raises one of his thick brows.

"Kevin and Eleanor. Just watching them this trip... He's

super obvious about it, but she's subtle. But you can tell."

"What do you mean?"

"Just the little things." I think back to the way Eleanor stroked the small of Kevin's back absentmindedly, how he didn't even have to ask how she wanted her turkey, the small glances and knowing looks exchanged across the dining table.

"You're right," Hayden says. "We knew from the day my brother first brought her home, that Eleanor was the one for him. They were both in grade seven."

I wonder what that's like...to love someone so instantly and completely.

"I've only seen one other couple that was that in love," Hayden continues. "My parents."

My heart hitches in my throat, and I turn my body to him. I curse my stupid brain for never having the right words to say, for staying silent when he needs me the most.

"It sounds wrong," Hayden mumbles, "but I'm sort of glad they died together. They couldn't have survived this world without the other." His breath quivers.

"It silly how there's billions of people on Earth, and one person can make or break the world for you," I finally say. "Maybe it's stupid, but I sort of believe there's only one real love out there for everyone." I look down at my boots, crunching in the snow.

"What are you, some sort of die-hard romantic?"

"No," I say quickly. "I just think we might be happy with someone else, but it won't be like...y'know..."

"Al, you might be right," Hayden says. "Somehow, it's just gotta all come together."

My chest feels heavy, and I stare upward at the sky. Somehow, amid this madness of stars, we got to be right here, right now...together.

I know when I get deep in thought, I forget to deepen my voice, or I'll cross my ankles or try to twirl my hair. And yet, these moments when I'm alone with Hayden are when I feel the most myself. The truest form of Alice I could possibly be.

And yet, he doesn't even know my real name.

"You know what?" I whisper. "I feel like all this chaos has spit me out exactly where I need to be." I turn to meet his eyes. "I know it will for you, too."

He takes a deep breath but doesn't look away. "Maybe it just has."

Chapter Thirteen

Carpets vacuumed: check.

Dishes washed and dried: check.

Laundry neatly folded: check.

Fresh sheets for both Ma and Xander's bed: check.

Floor gleaming so brightly I can see my sweaty face in it: check.

I fall back against the couch, more exhausted than after an overtime period. I don't think I've ever cleaned so much in my life. I even made sure to follow the special instructions on all of Xander's fancy shirts when I washed them! I've always believed if something doesn't survive the dryer, it doesn't deserve to be in my closet. Maybe that's why Xander's always had nicer clothes than me.

I look around at all my hard work. The house is eerily quiet now, without me clomping around. The clock on the mantle hits 6 p.m. I finished just in time—Ma and Xander will be home from the airport any minute.

I take a moment to breathe before real life begins again. It's been so weird, coming home from Winnipeg to an empty house. My heart feels heavy with each beat. I miss Hayden.

And I miss Mom and Xander, too.

I look at all the photos hanging on the walls and framed along the mantle: Mom with each baby in an arm, her pulling us on a sled when we were just toddlers, Xander and I heading into the ice rink as kids. There's even a picture of us sitting on the beach in Mexico from our Christmas vacation last year.

My throat and chest tighten. I couldn't go this year... I couldn't miss practice or a game. I wasn't being selfish! It was for Xander's cause!

I slouch down on the couch. Despite how many times I tell myself this, I know it's all just an excuse for the truth. I'm having a better time being Al than Alice, and no matter how many dishes I scrub, it won't change things. I ditched my mom and brother at Christmas.

The door swings open and Ma heaves her knock-off Louis Vuitton suitcase through the door. I jump up and snatch her other bags from her.

"Welcome home," I say.

"Hello, darling! Oh, thank you. That one's heavy."

Ma's face is gorgeously tanned—the rest of her is covered in a huge scarf and jacket to protect her from the mean Chicago wind.

Xander follows from behind her: his face is red and scorched, with flaking skin around the sides of his nose. My first instinct is to laugh hysterically, but for some reason, I can't bring myself to tease him. He looks so sullen, so weary.

Shyly, I stand back as Mom and Xander drop their bags in the hallway.

"Alice, what happened in here?" Ma says. "Did you hire an army?"

"No! I just thought I'd tidy up a little, that's all."

"It's sparkling!"

"Did you have a good time?" I ask.

Mom begins the long process of removing her winter layers. "Oh, yes, it was lovely. They've built a few new cabanas on the beach that are just to die for. But you have to get there right at the crack of dawn to get one to yourself. Why, one time I had to fight this Texan lady who thought she could just muscle her way in—"

I look at Xander and crack a smile. I can only imagine how awkward that must have been for him...but he's not smiling at me or rolling his eyes behind Ma's back like I expected. He just stares at his shoes. Although he's out of his cast, he still favors his weak side.

"—and she never tried that again!" Ma says, finishing the story I mostly zoned out for.

I look back at her and affect a smile. "Glad you guys had a great time."

"Well, we missed you, Alice," Ma says. She doesn't make eye contact with me, and my chest pangs painfully.

"I missed you guys, too," I say quietly.

"How was Winnipeg?" Ma asks as she walks to the couch.

I gulp. I'd hoped she wouldn't ask. I'd told her I was spending a few days with my teammate Hayden in Winnipeg. It wasn't my fault she'd just assumed Hayden was a girl. Of course, she had wanted all my details (flight times and the address I was staying at), but she really hadn't asked that much. I think she was still sore I wouldn't go to Mexico.

"It was really fun. I ate a ton of good food and played in the snow, and we even skated on a homemade ice rink!" No lies. I turn to Xander. "How are—"

"I'm going to take a shower." Xander turns without even looking at me and storms up the stairs.

"I think he really missed you," Ma says, nodding toward his bedroom. "He was pouting all week."

My stomach roils. What am I supposed to do if Xander won't tell me what's wrong? He was the one who lied to *me*. "No idea what's up with him. Bad taco, maybe."

Mom sighs audibly. "He'll get over it. He always does. Remember how quiet and moody he got right before we moved? Then when we arrived, he was a brand new person!"

Mom's right—Xander's moods are more unpredictable than Chicago's weather. "Hey, I got something for you." I pull out a small gift bag I hid behind the armchair. "Just a little something from Winnipeg."

Mom raises an eyebrow and takes the present hesitantly. "For me?" She reaches into the bag and pulls out a fat black bear stuffie.

"It's Winnie-the-Pooh," I explain. "Well, kind of. The bear that Winnie-the-Pooh was based on lived in Winnipeg like a million years ago. He's like a local icon there." I had bought it at one of the gift shops at the airport. When Hayden saw me with it, he went and bought one for himself.

"I'll give it to the baby," he had said.

Mom doesn't take her eyes off the stuffed bear. "I love it."

"I got a sweater for Xander, but maybe I'll give it to him later," I mumble.

"Don't fret about him." Mom caresses one of the little bear's ears. "Perhaps next year we could try something different. We could rent one of those chalets in Aspen or see the tree lighting in Nantucket. Or even just stay here. Just somewhere where there's snow." She gives me a cheeky look. "And ice, of course."

I lean my head on Ma's shoulder. "What, and have me go another year without seeing those new cabanas? No way."

• • •

"Zzz…but I wanna see the dinosaur people…zzz…"

A hand grabs my knee, and I shoot awake. "Al, wake up! We're here," Madison says. "Hello, Milwaukee!"

I rub my eyes. Harsh florescent lights blare overhead, and I see the blurry shapes of my teammates making their way off the bus. Jeez, I'm exhausted. From practices, games, rehearsing my figure skating routine for the approaching Ice Ball, homework, and navigating the never-ending minefield of Xander's emotions, it's been an exhausting couple of weeks. My Christmas vacation seems like a faraway dream.

"I guess I slept the whole way," I mutter and rub the goose bumps from my arms. I'm sure the whole left side of my face is red from being pressed up against the window for hours. It's good though; I know I won't be getting a lot of sleep tonight, figuring I promised Madison we'd hit up the house party of one of her friend's who lives in the city. I even packed a bunch of my girlie things—my hair extensions, a dress, a push-up bra even!—so I can be myself for a night. Or at least a dolled-up version of myself.

"Come on, Al!" Madison calls from the front of the bus. "You're the last one off!"

I give a big yawn and sling my bag over my shoulder. I feel like a zombie. Thank goodness Madison will be doing all the work to turn me back into a girl.

I can already feel the cool wind outside as I step toward the door of the bus, and hear the happy chatter of my teammates.

"A-Al!" Madison stutters, as I'm just about to step off. She stares at me, eyes wide, mouth open. "You, uh, lost something…" She points to her chest.

I look down and…my bandeau is gone! I look back and see a trail of medical tape on the floor of the bus. It must have come loose when I was passed out. Horrified, I stare down at my white T-shirt.

"Oh shit," I mutter. "Thank God everyone is off the bus—"

Footsteps clomp on the stairs. A voice.

Hayden's face peeks through the door. "Hey, Al!"

"EEE!" Madison screams and lurches forward, pushing me onto the nearest seat. She smothers me with her small body.

"Everything okay in..."

I hear Hayden's voice trail off as he gets to the top of the bus. But I can't see him as my face is buried in Madison's super shiny, blueberry-smelling hair.

I blink blankly, but thankfully Madison can think for two of us. "Oh sorry, Tremblay, I've been distracting your roomie."

I peer out from the dark curtain of Madison's hair and see Hayden standing there, wide-eyed. He gives an awkward grimace.

"I'll, uh, catch up in a moment," I say, hoping he doesn't notice how awkwardly I'm holding Madison's waist, or how much she's pressed against my chest.

"You two?" he finally says. "I never would have—"

Madison gives a high-pitched giggle and pinches my cheek. "This guy's just so cute! I can't help myself."

I give the bro-iest laugh I can muster. Shit, what do guys say about girls they like? God knows Freddy and Xander weren't good examples. "Ahh, my Maddy...she's one foxy lady."

Hayden looks like he's about to die. Or vomit.

I guess that's not what guys say.

"Ugh, you can have the room," Hayden groans, and walks off the bus. "I'm gonna go out with Sacs tonight."

We let out a collective sigh as soon as he leaves, and Madison immediately goes to work scooping up the medical tape and rebinding me.

"Hey, at least that got you off the hook about what to do with Mr. Grouchy!" Madison says cheerfully.

I should be happy Hayden said he won't be in our room tonight; after all, it will make sneaking around as a girl a lot easier. But instead, my stomach feels like I just dropped a thousand floors. What does it matter if Hayden goes out with Sacs tonight, finding pretty puckbunnies to hook up with? I can't ever be more than a friend to him.

I'm a boy. I'm Al.

And even if he knew the truth...why would he ever like a liar like me?

· · ·

"You look like it's your first time on skates." Madison raises her perfectly painted eyebrow at me.

"I was never this unsteady on skates," I say as I wobble around on the five-inch heels Madison made me wear. I make my way to the punch table, careful to take smaller steps in my short red dress. It's Madison's, and it's beautiful...and probably a perfectly respectable dress on her 5'2" body. But on me, it ends up just covering the top of my thighs and is wire-tight across my bust to accentuate what little chest I do have. Whatever magic Madison's done to me appears to be working, as one partygoer stops to ogle me.

I stare him down, so when he eventually flicks his eyes up to mine, he knows he's been caught. I muster the nastiest glare I can manage, but instead of looking embarrassed, he just grins at me. "Those are some legs on you."

Maybe all the makeup and false eyelashes and fake hair I have on are hiding just how menacing my glare can be. I'll have to work on that. I eye him carefully. I guess some people would think he's cute...okay, most people. He's got short-cropped hair and pale blue eyes, and he's tall...but not as tall as Hayden. Granted, not many people are.

He steps closer to me, his eyes running a line down my body. I wish I had my Falcons jersey on, because my skin is turning every shade of pink. I mutter something about finding my friend, sloppily pour myself a glass of punch, and lose myself in the crowd to find Madison.

The house is dimly lit and packed with people: mostly hockey players by the looks of it.

Madison spots me and grabs my arm. "What are you doing? He was cute."

I look over at the dude, who's already moved onto a new girl. "Not really my type."

"Why, because he doesn't wear plaid and play for the Falcons?"

I open my mouth to say something, but all I can manage is a wheezing sound. "Hayden is not my type! Yeah, I know he's good looking with his wavy brown hair, his dark eyes, his smile that lights up...." I trail off and look down at my drink. "But he's completely unreasonable, has a temper, and from all the stories I've heard from Daniel and Tyler, he's a complete manwhore! Plus, I've only had one boyfriend..." I stop talking, not wanting to think of Freddy right now.

"Yeah, yeah, Alice," Madison says. "You can make that list go on as long as you like, but you're still gonna blush whenever he's within fifty feet of you. And besides, he doesn't seem like he's getting around much this season. Has he tried to bring any girls back to the hotel?"

I tug the ends of my dress down. "No...if you don't count me." I smirk. I guess I've been doing a good job on following Coach's orders to keep Hayden out of trouble. And it doesn't seem like he's seeing anyone in Chicago—I would know. I spend a lot of weeknights just chilling at his house, doing homework or watching bad TV. It's easier to be there, away from everything, than to deal with Xander and Mom's constant judgment that I'm just not trying hard enough.

At Hayden's, even though I'm pretending to be a boy, it feels like I don't need to mold myself to meet someone else's expectations. I can say whatever I want, eat whatever I want, and—as ironic as it sounds—just be myself.

Plus, Xander's clothes are really comfy.

"Hey." Some guy taps Madison on the shoulder. He's got a bright smile and hair as red as my dress. "I'm looking for a partner in beer pong. Want in?"

Madison turns, slowly taking his hand off her shoulder. "No." He doesn't move, so she raises her voice and waves. "Bye!" The guy saunters off but keeps looking back at her.

Now it's my turn to raise an eyebrow at her. "*He* was cute."

She shrugs.

"I think you must like someone, too." I smile. "I mean… not *too*. I don't like anyone. You do!"

She laughs and sips her drink, but the color on her cheeks tells me I'm onto something.

I pinch her arm. "You like Xander!"

Madison bursts out laughing, her drink dribbling down her chin. "Xander?!" She clutches her side, doubling over.

"What's so funny?" I cross my arms. "I know I'm biased, but he's cute, and before he broke his leg, he was a pretty decent human being."

She looks up at me, chest still heaving with laughter. "Oh sweetie, I know. He's adorable." She tilts her head at me, like I'm a child. "You were…serious?"

"Um…yeah!" I cross my arms. "I think you guys would be cute together."

"I can't have this conversation when I'm sober." She looks down at her empty cup. "I'm gonna get a refill."

Madison walks over to the punch table. I don't know why she can't admit she likes Xander. She spends a lot of time at my house, and when she's not at the rink, she's always at the theater with Xander. And maybe getting a girlfriend would knock Xander out of his sour mood.

That redhead from earlier comes up to Madison, wrapping his arm around her waist. He's certainly getting more aggressive. But before Madison has time to dump her drink over that guy, which she seems to be preparing to do, someone comes over, forcefully removing the redhead's hand from her waist.

He's the tallest one in the room, with slicked black hair and a nose broken one too many times. Daniel Sacachelli. After Red scurries away, Daniel slips his own arm around Madison's waist. "If I just stand here all night, you won't have to deal with any of these creeps."

Madison rolls her eyes but doesn't push him away. "Yeah, because you're the king of creeps." Her head lolls onto his chest.

Daniel? She chose Daniel over Xander? But before I can fathom her reasoning, I spot a flash of strawberry-blond hair in the other room. Tyler Evans. I freeze. Suddenly, everyone in this room is suspicious. If Tyler and Daniel are here, that must mean Hayden's around; they were all going out tonight.

A wave of disappointment settles in my belly when I don't see him in the crowd. *Don't be stupid, Alice.* Out of all the Falcons, Hayden has the best chance of discovering my lie.

I have to get out of here.

As soon as I dart for the door, Madison rushes over and grabs my arm. "Hey, where do you think you're going?"

"If Daniel and Tyler are here, it means Hayden is, too. I can't let him—" Being Alice in front of Hayden as a figure skater was one thing. I had a mission. A plan. A routine. And there was no way out of it. But here, I have a clear escape route.

"Y'know, you could—" Madison says, clasping her hands

behind her back, "—just tell him."

My jaw nearly drops to the floor. Is she kidding? Tell Hayden? That what, I've been lying to him for the last five months, and hey, I've had the hots for him the whole time, too? I cross my arms and laugh. "And have Xander kill me? No thanks."

Madison shakes her head and looks back at Daniel at the punch table. Thankfully, he doesn't look over at us.

"I'm gonna get some rest before tomorrow's game." I force a smile. "Keep the boys from getting into too much trouble!"

She smiles at me. "I'm on it, Bell."

I twinge of sadness hits me as I wait outside for a cab. I can see Madison and Daniel through the window. She flicks her long black hair and laughs at everything he says, while he hasn't taken his eyes off her for a second.

I shake away the heaviness in my chest. No point mulling over what I don't have. It's time to take Alice off and turn back into Al.

• • •

HAYDEN

I take another sip of the wine bottle, realize it's empty, and drop it to the carpet with the other one. Stupid mini fridges and their stupid tiny bottles. At least they have variety. I crack the top off the Gray Goose and flip the channel.

Pathetic. Milwaukee is always known for having the best house parties. I know there's a howler going on now, and I should be there with Sacs and Evans, picking up girls and kicking ass at beer pong. But I just didn't feel like it. Better for me to stay in and rest up for the game tomorrow. I thought I'd just treat myself to one drink, or two...

I burp and take another swig of vodka.

I guess a part of me hoped Al didn't want to go either, and we could just chill together. Catch a movie, maybe. We've seen a couple movies at home in Chicago and he always laughs at the inappropriate parts, which makes me laugh.

But ever since we arrived in Milwaukee, he's been with Miranda. Or Madeline. Or whatever that trainer intern's name is. So I thought better of going out all night. Why should I be kicked out of my own room just so he can get laid? Who knew Al even had it in him!

I down the rest of the vodka in a single gulp. I guess I should be a better friend to Al...but I just don't have it in me right now. We're supposed to be helping each other out, not banging randos. Not that Mackenzie is even a rando. But if Al and Marina burst through this door ready to screw each other, I'm gonna tell them to get a room.

A different room.

I look at the clock. It's after midnight and still no sign of Al.

I know I should go to bed, but I open the mini rum instead.

Bzzup.

I hear the key card click and the door opens. I lean forward, ready to tell Al off for ditching me for some girl.

But it's not Al.

It's some girl.

Holy shit. I must be drunker than I thought; I'm hallucinating. Because there's no way some smoking hot girl in a tight red dress just walked into my room.

She looks as shocked as I feel, her big eyes darting out of her head. She starts to back away but stumbles on her high heels, barely catching herself on the door handle.

"W-wait!" I say, and brush the Pringles crumbs off my bare chest.

"Uh, sorry, uh—" She fumbles with the doorknob.

Damn, she is beautiful. Long, flowing brown hair, mile-long legs...even the deer-in-the-headlights look is endearing. And her eyes—

Damn. I know her.

"Alice?" I breathe.

My eyes trail over her familiar face, down her long neck and exposed collarbone, to the top of her red dress, so tightly hugging her chest.

She stares at me, then looks down, obviously making the connection between my eyes and her chest. Shit! What's wrong with me? I can't be checking out Al's sister!

"What are you doing here?" I say.

And then I notice her eyes doing the exact same thing mine were doing: they trail across my face, over my shoulders, down my bare chest, and to my boxers. I lean back. Hey, maybe it's rude to look, but that doesn't mean I can't give her an eyeful.

"I'm, uh, I'm here for the game," she finally says, her face growing bright red. "Here to watch Xander play the game. The game that is hockey."

"Al!" I say, straightening. She bristles at my enthusiasm. "Where is that little twerp anyway?"

"He's, uh..." She chews on her lip, only a pointed canine visible. Just like Al.

"Were you out with him and the trainer?" I start shoving shit off the bed. Empty alcohol bottles, chip containers, the works.

"Yeah, Madison." Her eyes dart around the room, almost as if she's looking for something.

"Where are they? Back in her room?"

"Uh, yeah, yeah, that's good!" She shakes her head. "I mean, I was supposed to be staying with Madison, but they were busy in her room. Xander said nobody would be in here."

"Sorry to disappoint." I grin. I can't let her wander around the hotel all night. "I'm just chilling, if you wanted to hang out." I pat the empty space on the bed beside me. "Thirsty?" I reach down and grab another one of the wine bottles.

Her startled face turns into another recognizable one— that twisted, constipated look Al gets when he's thinking too hard. Jesus, they're eerily similar.

Slowly, she walks toward me and plops down. "Pass me a glass."

"Yes, ma'am." The red wine rushes into the glass like the blood in my veins. I don't know why, but my heart pounds and my hands are slick.

Chill, Tremblay. I've had plenty of girls sit beside me in hotel rooms before. Beautiful girls, even. So what's different about this one?

I sneak a glance over at her. She sits awkwardly still, eyes unblinking at the unfunny late night comedian on the TV.

"So, Alice," I say, "what do you do?"

She turns to me, her head as stiff as a vampire's arising from a coffin. "What do I…do?"

"You know…" I look down. "Like what's your thing? Like mine and Al's is hockey…and the trainer's is…training…and Coach Z's is yelling."

Damn, she's got Al's pained grimace face down to a T. "I…I'm a figure skater." She looks down. Man, she must be nervous, because it sounded like every word was a struggle.

I can't help it… My eyes trail over her lithe body, down those endless legs. Her calves are toned and muscular. I remember how close I got to her on the ice and desperately wish to be that close again.

Ugh, Al would kill me if he knew I was ogling his sister right now.

But who cares? He left for a night out on the town with

his girl. Why shouldn't I have some fun too?

"Why are you looking at me like that?" Alice snaps.

I should apologize. I should excuse myself and let her have the room. I should at least put some pants on, for Christ's sake. Instead, I tell the truth. "You're really freaking pretty."

Boom. Those eyebrows shoot up, just like I knew they would. Her thin lips form a perfect O. "Who?"

I take the wine glass from her shaking hand and put it on the ground. "Cheers."

In an instant, I lace my hand through her hair and kiss her. Kiss her with everything I've got. Maybe it's the alcohol. Maybe it's loneliness. Or maybe it's those goddamn eyes, but damn, I want to kiss her.

At first, she doesn't do anything. She doesn't kiss me back, but she doesn't pull away, either. So I kiss her with more hunger, more urgency, more desire.

She responds like a cannon, grabbing my head and knotting her hands through my hair. I run my hands across her jaw, her collarbone, down her arms and the length of her waist. I want to touch every inch of her—my mouth craves to be on her lips, her neck, over the crest of her chest.

I don't know where to put my hands—I want to touch, kiss, and look at her, all at once.

Alice pushes on my chest, slamming me against the headboard, and attempts to straddle me, but her tight-fitting dress won't let her spread her knees far enough apart.

"Goddamn this thing," she snarls.

My fists clench and unclench, and I try to steady my breathing. "Alice, you are so sexy—"

She jams a finger against my lips. "Don't talk." With a throaty growl, she heaves the dress up to her waist, revealing a pair of black boyshorts. The way they hug her body... They're hotter than anything I've seen made of lace or silk.

And then she kisses me again, pressing her body against

mine with a passion I've never felt before. Her mouth is hungry, desperate even, as if she's been waiting to do this for a thousand years.

And damn, if I knew kissing her would be like this, I would have knocked down every door to find her. I tear myself away from her mouth and kiss my way up her jawline to her ear. "Where have you been the last few months, Al?"

Her body stiffens like a corpse.

. . .

ALICE

Which Al is he talking to?

Is he talking to Alice Bell, the washed-up female hockey player, the terrible sister and daughter, and the biggest idiot of the century for making out with her stinking hot teammate who doesn't know she's pretending to be a boy?

Or is he talking to Al Bell, number 44, right-wing for the Chicago Falcons, who leads the team in assists and shoot-out goals, and, oh yeah, is also secretly a *girl?*

I fling myself off his chiselled body and to my feet. My stupid red dress still clings to my waist, and hastily, I pull it down.

What am I thinking?

I bury my face in my hands and stumble backward, as if somehow that could reverse the last half-hour. How could I let myself fall for Hayden Tremblay? And not just fall for him on the ice, but here, where I'm vulnerable to his ploys and plays. He's wanted me for thirty minutes, and I've wanted him for five months.

I'm such an idiot.

"Everything okay?" he says, reaching forward.

I lurch out of reach. "Don't touch me!"

"D-did I do something?" Concern flickers across his

face, and my heart hurts. Ugh, he looks so sweet sitting there, his brow upturned and his hair mussed up. And God, it's so sexy knowing I'm the one who mussed it.

I have to get out of here.

"No, I just—" I turn away, unable to continue. I spot my— or Al's—duffle bag half-shoved in the closet and hoist it up over my shoulder. "I forgot I have to go."

"Wait, Alice!"

"You weren't supposed to be here," I whisper. "Just forget this ever happened. Please."

I walk toward the door, barely able to contain my shattered breath. I have to leave. For Xander. For the team.

And for Hayden. For Hayden most of all.

"Good-bye, Tremblay."

· · ·

I jam my finger against the elevator button a thousand times, as if it could make it come faster. When I finally get inside the damned thing, each wall is a mirror, and I'm surrounded by four different Alices.

I am a mess.

The eight-million pounds of makeup have run down my face, my hair is a tangled nest, my dress is wrinkled and uneven, and the only thing that looks in place is Al's bag flung over my shoulder.

I stagger out into the lobby and into one of their large public washrooms.

I kissed Hayden. Hayden kissed me!

The thought travels through me like a wave, and that's when I start to cry. Not a nice, dainty cry, but a full-on ugly sob. I push into a stall and lock the door, but I can't stand. I fall to the bathroom floor.

What *was* that? What does it mean? Why do I feel it in

every part of me?

Guilt floods through me. Xander will never forgive me if he realizes how much I've risked. And Hayden...the thought is too painful.

A small knock sounds on the door, and one of the hotel staff gingerly asks if I'm all right. She asks what room I'm staying in, and I cry even louder—because there's no room here for Alice Bell.

Who am I? Some girl sobbing on the bathroom floor. This is definitely not something Al Bell does, but it's not something Alice does either. Alice never cries, especially over a boy. Over anything.

I stop sobbing for a moment, tell the lady I'll be out in a moment, and think. I can't even remember the last time I cried.

I was five years old when Mom sat us down and said Dad had left and he wasn't coming back. All three of us cried that day. And then I never cried again. On special occasions like Father's Day or birthdays, when Xander would go and shut himself in our bedroom, I would be totally fine. Mom would tell me it's okay to be sad.

I don't even know if I'm sad now.

I just feel lost.

I stand up and decide that's a start. I throw off my dress and bra, wrap my boobs, and throw on Al's hoodie and sweatpants.

Then I stand in front of the mirror and put away Alice. I take out all the fake hair, wash the makeup off my face, rip off my fake eyelashes and throw them in the trash—even though they cost over nine dollars.

I look in the mirror and see Al. I thought I'd feel a little better. A little more certain.

But now, I'm even more lost. I don't even know who Al is. But the scary part is...in becoming Al, I think I've lost

Alice too.

I don't know who I used to be.

And I most certainly don't know who I am.

. . .

I don't know how long I've been waiting in that bathroom—at least an hour, maybe two—but it should be enough time for Hayden to be asleep. All I want to do is slip into my bed and forget this ever happened. I drag my feet up to the room, and when I open the door, I'm bathed in light. And the smell of vomit.

I look around the room. The sheets of his bed are a tangled mess, and there's a calamity of empty booze bottles on the ground: way more than when I was here as Alice.

Some pathetic moans travel out from the bathroom, and I poke my head in. There he is, sprawled across the toilet, shivering and absolutely pathetic.

He turns to me slowly, barely makes eye contact, and then returns to the toilet.

Nasty.

"Hang in there, buddy," I murmur. I wet a cloth with hot water and wipe his mouth. No point worrying about if this is something "bros" would do—he won't remember this tomorrow. Then I go to the mini fridge and pull out a bottle of water, unsurprisingly full, and his sweatshirt and pajama pants. "Let's get you ready for bed, dude."

He leans against the bathtub. Hopefully he's barfed up all his guts for the night. I hand him his sweatshirt and pants.

After a pathetic attempt, he's got his pants on, but one arm through the head hole of his shirt. He falls limp against the tub. "Al, I'm dying."

I pull the sweater over his head. "You're not dying," I mutter. "You're just an idiot."

Hayden collapses on my shoulder and laughs a little. The sound sends blood racing through my veins. He doesn't look quite so disgusting now; his hair falls across his eyes, and he gives big, sleepy blinks. Not so pathetic...just fragile.

He looks up at me, his dark eyes narrow. A furrowed brow and pursed lips make him look like he's thinking...

"Al," he mutters. And in the space of the breath, I imagine him saying a million different things. The world suddenly opens up a chasm of possibilities. He could say anything. He could *know*. I could tell him the truth right now. The truth. And something else hangs there too—but I'm not quite sure what it is yet.

"Yeah?" I whisper and I'm not sure if I sound like Alice or Al, or if there's even a difference right now.

He looks at me for a moment longer, then smiles a little. "Y'know, you're my best friend."

You're my best friend.

A sad smile crosses my face.

That'll do.

I sniff, and a tear whispers down my cheek.

And that thing—that elusive *thing* that was hanging in front of me—suddenly becomes clear. And all the possibilities, well, they all point to it.

You've done it now, Bell.

I've fallen in love.

Chapter Fourteen

ALICE

"I'm so TIRED." I practically collapse as I walk through the front door.

"Stop your whining, Alice," my mother clips. "It's not ladylike."

I throw my figure skating bag on the floor and let loose the biggest moan I can manage. Mom doesn't have eight pounds of fake hair weighing on her neck. Mom doesn't have to manage high school and figure skating rehearsals and hockey practice, all while pretending to be a boy and a girl at the same time. I moan again, louder this time.

The days have all turned into a blur. Coach has intensified practices now that the playoffs are right around the corner. And for the first time in a few years, the Falcons have a chance to make them. Then there's Mom's charity Ice Ball, which is coming up soon too! I haven't even thought about how I'm going to keep Alice, the figure skater, away from all the Falcons, who are supposed to attend...or why Al won't be there. As long as I don't run into Hayden, it should be okay. He's the only one who might have a chance of recognizing me as, well, me.

A sharp jab of shame sits in my chest as my mind drifts back to that night in the hotel room. Hayden never said anything to Al about Alice and never tried to contact me again. It's clear that night was nothing but an attempt at a one-night stand.

I stumble up the stairs, whacking my bag on each step. I've got about half an hour before the hockey game. Most of that will be spent washing off Alice and becoming Al.

Trudging into my bedroom, I collapse on my bed. If I close my eyes for even a second, I might fall asleep. That's when I notice Xander, sitting at my computer desk.

"Hey," I mumble, face half-buried in my pillow. "What are you doing?"

He spins around slowly. "I had to print my research paper for school."

I close my eyes. I'm about done with Xander and his emo self lately.

"You left your pictures up."

My eyes pop open. I'd uploaded all my pictures from Christmas vacation. Xander clicks on a selfie of Hayden and me. He was making me try this weird Canadian food with squeaky cheese on French fries. It was amazing.

"Don't freak out," I say, sitting up. "Look at the pictures. I look just like you." Same scraggly hair, the deep smile, the round eyes. "I was so careful the entire time. No one knows. No one could tell us apart."

"That's the point, Alice! No one can tell!"

I get up and slam the laptop screen down. "What's your problem?"

He crosses his arm and glares at me. I've been pretending to be him for so long, it's almost like looking in a mirror.

"You spend all your time with him...on and off the rink. You went to his freaking hometown! And you talk about him all the time!"

I recoil. "So what, I'm not allowed to have friends now, huh?"

"Except he's not just your friend," Xander says, his words harsh and cutting. "You love him."

His words strike me like a check against the boards. Because Xander is right. I do love Hayden Tremblay. And I want him more than anything I've ever wanted before. I want to watch him lose himself on the ice, and be there to feel his energy during a game, and see him grow into the leader he was meant to be. I want to be with his family and hear their silly stories and eventually remember all their names. And I want to sit with him in a snow bank staring at ghosts until we've chased them all away.

And as much as it hurts to admit it, I want Hayden to see me as a girl, to feel his body against mine, to kiss those lips like I did in the hotel room. I love him.

So I tell Xander part of the truth. "It doesn't matter how I feel. I'm a *boy* with him. He thinks I'm his best friend."

Xander shakes his head, nervously clenching and unclenching his fists. "People talk, Alice. People are going to notice how close you guys are. It'll get around the league."

"That we're friends?" I raise my hands in disbelief. "I haven't heard anything!"

"You don't hear because you don't listen!" Xander yells. He stands, getting right in my face. "What they're saying isn't about Alice Bell! It's about me. But in Alice's world, only Alice matters!"

Anger flies through my body, and I pace around him. "You know what, Xander? I did hear something. I heard what Freddy said to *Alexander* Bell. You knew he was cheating on me. You knew, and you never told me! I'm your sister! How could you?"

His face drops, fading of all color and emotion. "It wasn't supposed to be like this."

"It doesn't matter, Xander," I spit. "You betrayed me, to keep some secret of your own. You think I'm being selfish? You're the selfish one. Because I do pay attention to Alexander Bell. I pay attention every time *Alexander Bell* is checked into the boards and every bone in my body rattles. When *Alexander Bell's* stats go up every time I score a goal. How scouts are now saying *Alexander Bell's* name when I step on the ice. Those are the things I pay attention to."

"Al—" Xander argues, but I storm out of the room.

• • •

HAYDEN

The locker room buzzes with energy. Home game against our rivals, the Ice Wolves, and we're on a winning streak. I jog in place to try and get some of the anxious energy out of my body. We just need a few more wins to get into the playoffs—but a few losses could mean another worthless season.

Anger rises in me as I think about facing Galen Fredlund on the ice. He thought I hit him hard back at the bonfire? Hah. I hardly knew Alice then. If I could get my hands on him now—

I stop myself. I can't go down this path. Fighting with Fred will only hurt the Falcons and thinking about Alice will only hurt me. She's Al's *sister*. And that's a line I'm not prepared to cross. That night in the hotel room…well, it will just have to stay a memory.

At least I'll get to see Fredlund's face when he gets humiliated in front of our crowd.

As usual, Al's already here, dressed in the blue Falcon uniform. He's always here, ready to go, way before anyone else. He's got more quirks than anyone I know: the way he always has to be ready before anyone else, his weird allergy to soap, the way he's always clearing his throat... Even though he's a freak, I smile when I sit down beside him.

"How ya doing, eh?"

Al doesn't respond. His eyes are glassy, and his mouth is a thin straight line.

"Al?"

"I'm fine. Just thinking." He hasn't blinked once since I sat down.

"Well, don't hurt yourself." I laugh and give him a shove.

"Stop!" Anger fills his voice, and he pushes my hand away. "Just...don't, okay?"

"Whatever, man."

I heave a sigh of relief as Coach Z walks in. I'll deal with Al's mood swings later.

Coach Z's eyes are intense under his heavy eyebrows. He stands in front of us, arms crossed, and stares each of us down. He locks eyes with me a moment longer than anyone else, but a small smile appears under his thick moustache. *What are you planning, Coach?*

"Well, boys, it's been a hell of a season. We've played together for months now, and taken some hard losses. But we've had some triumphant wins, too. As a coach, I couldn't be more proud of how you've grown as a team. Not only our new players, who joined us at the beginning of the season, but our veteran players too. You've worked together, found connections, and kicked ass. All of you have committed to the bird."

His eyebrows rise, revealing smiling gray eyes. I don't think I've ever seen Coach look so...happy? "And maybe none so much as one particular player. A fierce playmaker, goal-scorer, team player, and leader. I'm proud to say that I finally feel confident to name the Falcons' captain."

Coach Z stares straight at me, and all my teammates follow his gaze. My stomach lurches back toward my spine. *Is this really happening?*

Coach grins and picks up a jersey emblazoned with a C. "Congratulations, Tremblay. You've earned it."

It almost feels like I'm walking through my own imagination as I jump up, surrounded by the hoots and hollers of my teammates. A smile breaks across my face. I probably look like an idiot, but I don't care. Coach shakes my hand and claps me on the back. I pick up the jersey and stare at it.

Tremblay. Captain Tremblay.

I can't wait to tell Kevin about this. A strange warmth fills me. I don't want to tell him just because I have something to prove. I want to tell him because I'm proud, and he's going to be happy for me.

I notice Coach Z holds two other jerseys as well.

"Sacachelli, Bell," Coach barks, grinning, "congratulations. You're now our new alternate captains. Keep Tremblay in line, won't you?"

Sacs jumps up with a howl and gives me a flying hug. I laugh and hand him his new jersey with the shiny white A. Wasting no time, he throws off his old jersey and whips on the new one.

Al hasn't even moved. He's still sitting there, staring off into the distance, that emotionless look on his face. He should have already been grinning from ear to ear because I got captain…he goddamn knows how much it meant to me. But Coach just named him an alternate! A complete rookie, getting the A! I expect him to be dancing around the locker room and embracing Coach in one of those awkward hugs he loves to give.

Coach clears his throat. "Uh, Alexander Bell is one of the new alternates."

Now the whole team looks at him. He stares down at his

skates.

I walk over and touch his shoulder. "Al?"

At my touch, he leaps up and looks around as if he just woke up from a thousand-year sleep and has never seen the inside of a locker room before.

"The jersey, yeah." A weak smile forces itself on his face, and he quickly grabs the jersey and sits back down. "Thanks."

Coach talks strategy for a few minutes, then we break before the game. I turn to Al. "How cool is this?"

He avoids eye contact. "Yup. It's cool."

"You gonna put it on?" I look down at his new jersey, hanging limply in his lap.

"In a minute."

I put my jersey on, savoring the feeling of the fresh linen sliding over my body. I want to feel pumped up, but something about Al's mood puts me on edge. "Everything okay, man?"

"It's *fine*," he snaps and stands up, too.

Maybe he's nervous about the game. I try some positivity: "Come on, this is awesome! I wonder what Fredlund and his pups will think when they see our new letters!"

"They'll probably wonder why it took so long for the Falcons to get a captain."

The words hit me like a puck to the chest. He meets my gaze, only then realizing what he's said. He tries to laugh it off: "Not that it matters when we cream them." But there's no laughter in his words.

I stare at him blankly, then head to the bench. The last thing I want is to get into a fight before the game. What's his problem? He knows how hard I've worked for this...how hard we've worked together.

I can't let it get to me. Maybe we both need to let off steam.

Thank God we're playing the Ice Wolves tonight.

...

ALICE

Jesus Christ, Alice. Get your head in the game.

Or Al.

Or whoever is holding this goddamn hockey stick right now.

These first two periods have been absolutely dismal. We can't keep the puck out of our zone and the Detroit Ice Wolves lead 3–0. But I can't think about anything except my fight with Xander.

How did I get in so deep?

Hey, everyone's allowed an off day. It should be Hayden, our new captain, carrying the team. But we can't land a pass between the two of us, and in-between shifts, he keeps looking at me like a wounded puppy. Dammit, he's a grown man, can't he take a little joke?

Except I didn't mean it as a joke, and he knew that.

I didn't mean to discredit Hayden. He really has worked hard this season. But it's his fault I'm in this scenario. It's his fault I couldn't just keep my head down and lay low with the team. Everything is all his fault!

The whistle blows, and Sacachelli heads to the box for tripping. Great, another power play for them.

I start to head to the bench when someone gives me a little shove from behind. I swivel on my skates and turn around to see Freddy's arrogant smirk.

"Can't land a pass, eh, Xander? What, too distracted by your pretty boy captain?"

I clutch my stick tighter. *Just ignore him.* But I can't. He blackmailed my brother. "What's your problem, Freddy? Keep your dumb lies to yourself, or I'll let all the teams know every injury you've ever had in your entire life!"

He spits and laughs, skating a little closer to me. "Lies, Xander? You're still trying to deny it? You think I'll forget all about when you asked out Ben Walker? I'll never forget that in a million years, you faggot!" He jerks forward and pushes me in the shoulder. "Now that Allie broke up with me, there's nothing to keep me from spilling your secret. Just you wait... When it'll hurt the most, that's when I'll tell."

I'm too shocked to move. Freddy leers at me, waiting for a reaction. But I don't have anything to give. My mind floods with memories.

Ben Walker used to be on our hockey team back home. Xander and him were pretty close, but right before we moved, they drifted apart. Is that what happened?

Is Xander gay?

I don't get time to dwell on it because Freddy, angered by my lack of reaction, rushes forward. "Don't you have anything to say for yourself, Bell?"

Suddenly, he shrinks back.

"He might not, but I do." Hayden skates up behind me.

Freddy shakes his head but keeps his gloves on. I guess he remembers the last time he and Hayden got in a fight. He grimaces, revealing a smile of chipped teeth. "Better watch yourself, Bell. You just picked the worst fight of your life!"

Freddy skates away, and I turn to Hayden. He shakes his head. "You gotta ignore him. Don't let him get under your skin."

"Hey," I mutter, biting down on my mouth guard, "you're starting to sound like me."

"Let's just focus on landing some passes, eh." He laughs and smiles down at me.

But his smile and laugh doesn't fill me with same happiness it usually does. Instead, it makes me feel...guilty.

How has this been for Xander? I played hockey because I wanted to play hockey. Because I wanted to prove I belonged here. And my friendship with Hayden...that was because...

My teeth grind so hard into my mouth guard, my jaw almost locks. I push it back into my mouth and look out at the ice. This isn't the time to think. This is the time to play hockey.

The next set starts, and Hayden's on fire, pushing hard against the Ice Wolves. Evans shoots a powerhouse of a shot that dings off the post. But no matter how hard I try, I can't sort out my thoughts. Hockey usually keeps my head straight, but I can't even keep my eyes on the puck.

Xander is gay?

Freddy could be lying but...now it seems like everything makes sense.

Xander is *totally* gay!

Why didn't he tell me? Or Mom? Or anyone? And no wonder he got mad about me spending so much time with Hayden. He's been trying to keep this secret his entire life and suddenly, I come along and glue myself to the hottest boy in all of Chicago!

"Heads up, Al!" Hayden calls, and shoots the puck toward me.

Somehow I manage to stick it. I'm pretty sure this is the first time I've touched the puck all night—

My bones shudder as I slam against the boards. A crack rings through the arena as the Plexiglas crumbles with the impact. Blinding pain shoots through my body as I smack against the ice, feeling shards of glass rain down.

Black spots dart in front of my vision. I hear people screaming, but it's muffled, like I'm underwater. There's a flurry of movement around me.

A face appears.

Hayden.

"Al! Al! Are you okay?"

There's only one answer I can give. If I'm not okay, it

means I'm injured. If I'm too badly injured, they'll take me to medical. They'll take off my jersey and see who I really am!

I squeeze my eyes shut. *Pull it together, Bell.* I open my eyes and manage to croak, "I'm fine."

I try to piece together the blurry shapes around me. Both refs and the linesmen are here, and my whole freakin' team— and they've surrounded Freddy, like a pack of lions around a baby wildebeest. Of course it was Freddy who checked me.

Check? It felt like a freight train. He hit me hard enough to shatter the glass.

"I just need to get to the bench." I sit up. Pain rips through me. "J-just help me up."

Hayden grabs me under my arms and helps me to my feet. I bite down on my mouth guard to keep from calling out. As we skate toward the bench, I look back to see all the trainers and first aid responders have gathered around the broken glass.

"Some of the fans are hurt," Hayden says. "They got cut by the glass."

Madison paces nervously on the bench and a wave of relief washes over me. I'll go with her while all the trainers are distracted.

I step onto the bench, staggering. My chest feels like it's about to rip open with every breath.

Coach grabs my arm. "How you doing, kid? What do you need?"

Two of his giant moustaches waver in front of my face. I try to focus, but all I can do is nod toward Madison.

She rushes forward and hooks an arm around me. "I'll look after him and make sure everything is okay!"

Coach nods, and we head toward the back.

"Al, wait! Are you okay?" Hayden jumps over the bench and heads toward us.

"We're fine, Tremblay," Madison says sternly. "Concentrate

on the game."

Hayden looks like a lost kid, staring helplessly at me as we round the corner into the back rooms.

As soon as we make it to the training room and lock the door, I collapse onto the medical bed and unravel. Tears flood down my face, and I cry out.

Madison's hands are all over my body, feeling my head, neck, arms. When she gets to my ribs, I scream.

"You're hurt," she shudders. "I need to get the doctor."

"No!" I shout. "They'll find out."

She sets her jaw, and I can see the unease in her eyes. "I need to take a look."

Carefully, she removes my helmet, jersey—my beautiful new jersey—skates, and equipment until I'm just in my black compression pants and top. Slowly, she sits me up so she can remove my tight undershirt.

I look down. A giant red bruise scrawls its away below my breast.

"Shoot, Alice," she whispers.

Loud bangs fill the room as someone hammers on the door. "Al, are you in here?"

Hayden. He sounds so worried.

Madison lets out a breath and walks over to the door. "Uh, the doctor is just doing an examination. Al's fine."

Hayden bangs on the door again. "Well let me in! Why is this even locked? Hey, Al! They're taking a break to clean up the glass!"

Madison shoots a look at me. Damn, he's persistent.

I cough and lower my voice, grimacing at the pain. "I'm good, man. Just, uh, go beat the Ice Wolves!"

"Let me in! You got hit so hard—"

"Tremblay! Get back to the game!" Madison snaps. "The doctor needs to concentrate."

A moment passes, and then footsteps echo. My heart

sinks. Out of everyone in the world, he's the one I want here with me now.

She walks back over, her eyes dark and narrowed. "You've got massive bruising. You may have broken a rib." I stare blankly at her until she says, "You need to go to the hospital."

"No, I can't!"

She sits beside me and smoothes down my hair. "Shush, don't worry. I'll go tell Coach it's nothing serious, but I'm going to take you to the hospital to make sure you don't have a concussion. Once we arrive there, you can check in as Alice Bell."

I nod. Some morphine sounds pretty good right now.

"Let me unbind you before we go. The pressure on your ribs could restrict your breathing." Madison's cool fingers carefully remove my tight bondage. I clamp my hands against the side of the bed. Damn, Freddy really got me. How could I not see him for who he was? A complete asshole who would blackmail his girlfriend's brother.

Guilt seeks deeper into me. My poor brother.

Goose bumps raise on my skin as Madison grabs a roll of gauze and lightly wraps it around my breasts and ribs. She stands back, admiring her work. "That should do until we get to the hospital. I'll go tell Coach."

"And grab my bag," I say. "I have my hoodie and phone in there."

Madison nods and leaves the room, locking the door on her way out.

I guess I'll have to let Mom know I'm in the hospital. She'll freak out that I got injured, but as long as this doesn't interfere with the Ice Ball, I think I'll manage to survive this.

I squeeze my eyes shut. This is okay. I will be okay. At least my head feels normal now, and I didn't break a wrist or ankle. My ribs will heal and I will play again.

But Xander—

The lock clicks and the door handle turns. "That was fast, Madison. Did you remember my bag—?"

My voice stops. It's not Madison standing in the doorway. It's Hayden.

• • •

HAYDEN

I can't think straight. It's not that there are no thoughts in my head—there are too many of them. And none of them make any sense.

I got the keys from Coach to go check on my teammate. My friend. Al Bell.

But that's not Al, sitting on the bed.

It's a girl.

She wears tight black Bauer pants and nothing on her top, except a loose bandage—across what is *very* clearly a chest.

Al doesn't have boobs. Al doesn't have legs like that. Or a voice like that.

Memories flash across my brain. Have I ever seen Al in anything besides his jersey or sweats and a baggy shirt? Is this even my friend?

"Get out!" the girl screams.

But I don't. I step inside.

"For fuck's sake! Close the door!" That voice. It sounds like Al now, that familiar nasally shriek. I close the door behind me, but I can't take my eyes off the person in front of me.

While it's not Al...it is. The same scruffy hair, the big gray eyes, that deer-in-headlights gaze. His jersey, pants, and skates lie on the floor.

"What's going on?" I say. There's anger in my voice. She doesn't respond. "Who are you?" I snap.

She looks down. "I-I'm… I'm Al Bell."

"Al's my teammate. Where's the real Al Bell?" I look around, as if my friend I saw getting hauled off the ice will suddenly appear.

"You've never met him!" she shouts. "My brother's name is Alexander Bell. He broke his leg right before the season began, so I pretended to be him. So he wouldn't lose his spot on the team."

I look at this stranger in front of me. None of this makes any sense. My body trembles with an anger I didn't know I was capable of. It hums under my skin like a living thing.

All the time I've spent with my friend Al…he's been a girl. I shake my head and refuse to believe it. I've spent almost every day with Al for the last few months. I would have known! This has to be some sort of sick joke, and my friend, the real Al, is going to come out and laugh.

But as I look at the girl in front of me, I know I'm wrong. She's the real Al.

"So…you've been lying to me this whole time?" I spit and put a hand on the door. "You're a liar."

"I'm Alice," she says. Her face twists in pain and she clutches her side. Suddenly, she falls forward and before I even know what I'm doing, I lurch forward to catch her.

She grimaces and shudders against my touch.

In my arms, she seems so small, so fragile. "Alice," I repeat, eyes searching her face, only inches from mine. Alice Bell. My dream girl from the hotel room.

"Y-you," I gasp, "you manipulated me."

A sad, terrible realization settles on me. This whole time, every moment I've spent with Al Bell, the person I thought was my best friend, has been a lie.

"Hayden, it wasn't—"

I put her back on the bed. She bends over, whimpering slightly. It hurts to look at her, but I can't seem to tear my eyes away. "I brought you to meet my family...I told you about my parents..."

"I-it wasn't a lie," she says through gritted teeth.

"Yes. It was." I turn my back on this stranger. "You need to go to the hospital."

"M-Madison's taking me."

I laugh. "You really thought this thing through. Fake girlfriend, fake name. Fake friend. You must have thought I was an idiot."

Somehow, she staggers off the bed and hobbles toward me. "Hayden, wait. I...I, um..."

I look down at her. She seems so tiny compared to me in my skates. What could she possibly say to explain all this? To justify lying to me all this time? Yet, deep down, a bubbling hope rises in my gut that maybe she'll be able to, that she'll tell me she didn't mean to make me a fool. Maybe there was some truth to our friendship after all.

"Yes...Alice?"

"You can't tell anyone."

"What?"

"No one can know I'm a girl. Please!"

My stomach sinks. Here I am, falling for her tricks again. How could I have thought she would be worried about what I would think? I may have thought Al Bell was my friend, but this stranger is concerned with only one thing. Herself.

My hands tighten into fists, and I have to look away. "Whatever."

"I couldn't tell you," she says finally. "I couldn't trust anyone!"

"Except Madison?"

"That was...different."

"Save it," I spit. "I don't care." I stare right into those damn familiar eyes and feel disgust rise in me. "You kissed me!" I avert my eyes, unable to look at her when I say it: "You kissed me!"

"That was a mistake…you weren't supposed to be there! Besides, you were drunk and you kissed me!" Her face flushes red.

So none of it meant anything to her. And now she reveals what she really thinks of me: just some drunk hockey player in a hotel room. "I bet you and Madison had a great laugh about that. Sad, pathetic Hayden Tremblay. I bet you thought sitting in the snow in front of my parent's ice rink was hilarious too."

"No," she says, and her voice cracks. "I didn't mean to get so close to you…to take it so far."

I close my eyes, suck in a deep breath, and then take a good long look at her. I can't see my friend Al anymore. I can't even see the girl from that hotel room, the one whose kiss always lingered in the back of my mind. I don't see anyone at all.

"Well, Alice Bell," I say, "I'm sorry I was such an inconvenience to you."

Her lips curl into a snarl. "None of this is about you, okay? You don't understand. Just, please, don't tell anyone." She grabs my hand. "Please, Hayden."

And it comes back to that. The true reason she's upset. Not that she lied to me for months. I wretch my hand away.

The door clicks open and Madison walks in. She looks frantically between Al —Alice— and me.

I mutter under my breath, "Don't worry, your secret's safe with me." I walk to the door. "It always would have been."

Chapter Fifteen

Madison locks the door and looks over at me. Her eyes are wary, as if she could break me with just a look. "Are you okay?"

"I'm fine," I say, surprised at how calm my voice is.

This is me, I think. This is the Alice I remember. The girl who was totally fine after watching Freddy cheat. The girl who watched her dad leave, then never cried a day after. The girl who can take hit after hit after hit on the ice and still get back up.

The other Alice, the lost one who sobbed on the bathroom floor after Hayden kissed her, and the distracted mess out on the ice a few minutes ago...well, there's not a trace of her left inside me.

There just isn't room.

Crying has never solved anything, and that distracted mess got hurt after being slammed up against the boards.

As Madison helps me put on my hoodie and sweats, I

catch her gaze. She's staring at me as if there's something wrong with me. Like, something wrong on the inside.

I take a few deep breaths as we make our way out of the arena. So what if Hayden found out my secret? It'll be okay. I'll call him. We'll have a long talk. He'll understand. He was just so riled up because a game was on. He's always like that during a game—edgy and unreasonable. After the game, I'll convince him to keep Xander's secret. My secret.

He'll understand.

He has to understand.

. . .

HAYDEN

They've replaced the Plexiglas, bandaged up the injured fans, and now we're due to resume play at any moment. Our team sits on the bench, tapping our knees anxiously. We're all eager to get this over with. Five minutes left in the game and we haven't even scored a goal.

Murmurs drift over the bench. A teammate out. They keep asking me if he's okay. What are his injuries? Will he be back next game?

I can't reply to any of them. What should I say? Pretty banged up ribs, nasty bruise, oh yeah, and now Al's a girl. My paranoid brain runs rampant — are any of my other teammates keeping things from me the way Al did?

I shake my head. It doesn't matter. None of them had what Al and I did...that chemistry on and off the ice. My mind flashes back to that insanely hot girl in the hotel room. How could she kiss me like that and then play with me the next day as if nothing had happened?

I try to merge the two people together: Alice and Al.

I just can't.

"Tremblay, you're up," Coach Z says. I stand, about

to jump over the bench when Coach puts a hand on my shoulder. "Bell's going to be all right. Myong's taking him to the hospital, just as a precaution."

Hearing Coach talk about Al makes me sick. He has no idea. Al was so damn sly. All his little tricks start to make sense: coming to games in full gear, being allergic to soap, that stupid nasally voice. All part of the lie.

I nod, but Coach doesn't let go of my shoulder. "I know Fredlund gave Bell a big hit, but the best way to make them pay isn't to hit back harder."

I try to move away, but Coach grips my jersey harder. I sigh and turn, until I'm eye to eye with him. Instead of anger, his face is full of concern. He really thinks I'm going to go out and start a fight with Fredlund. Coach doesn't realize Al isn't worth it. Why would I defend a liar like that?

"You're the captain now," he says. "Show them what that means."

I give another nod then dash onto the ice. What does it mean? Al was the one who helped me earn the C. We had a plan to make it happen. But none of that meant anything to him at all.

Her. To her at all.

Furious anger rises in me again. I tighten my grip on the stick and concentrate on the roar of the crowd. I skate to center ice, ready to take the faceoff. My whole body burns with violent energy. I need to play.

Fredlund skates across from me. My teeth grit and the image of him knocking into Al flashes across my vision. Somehow, his dirty check passed as legal, but I knew he was trying to hurt her.

My blood boils and I stare him down, daring him to say something. He meets my gaze with pale eyes and that smug look that tells me he knows exactly what he did.

"Crying that your little crony got hurt?" he sneers. "What

are you going to do without anyone to feed you goals?"

I breathe in and out, trying to remember Coach's words, but Fredlund's voice fills me with sick adrenaline.

He throws his head back. "What a sorry excuse for a captain! You should have seen your face when Bell went down. White as a ghost. Like you've never seen a hit before."

His words course through me, like he's filling me with toxic fuel. I give him a small smile, daring him to keep going. *It'll only make it worse for you.*

He darts his eyes to the ref, who skates toward us with the puck, then whispers just low enough for me to hear. "But that's not true. You've seen a big hit before, when you waved bye-bye to Mommy and Daddy."

The ref hovers with the puck between us. Fredlund wins the faceoff and scoots off down the ice.

I move without even reading the play. I don't realize what I'm doing until I'm almost on him. I skate faster. Fredlund passes the puck, and now it's on the other side of the rink.

It doesn't matter. He brought my mom and dad into this.

And he hurt Alice.

Fredlund wanted a fight…now he's going to get it. I slam into him as hard as I can. I've never been more ready for a fight in my entire life. But I don't get a chance. He sails forward and crashes face first onto the ice.

And doesn't get up.

Alice

"I'm not sitting in that," I say to Ma. She stands in the doorway of my hospital room, hands on the wheelchair. I shove past it and step into the hallway.

"It's only a few bruised ribs," I say. "Nothing's broken!"

"But the doctor said to be gentle, sweetheart!"

"Ugh, don't remind me." 'Be gentle' in doctor-speak means I'll be out for the next five games. Madison headed back to the rink to deliver the bad news to Coach. I hope he's not too upset, or reconsidering his decision to give me the A. Not that I did a single thing to earn it today.

Mom toddles up behind me and forces me to put on my winter jacket: a bright pink one with a faux fur trim that she bought me two Christmases ago. If I include today, this will make a grand total of one time that I've worn it.

I look at my mother. She scurried over here as fast as she could once I texted her I was in the hospital. Mascara is splotched around her eyes.

Oh no, her tears were not from seeing my pain or my bruised ribs.

It's from when she walked into the hospital room and saw my choppy bob.

Yes, my mother cried because I cut my hair. The only bright side of this entire day is knowing I'll never have to wear fake hair extensions ever again.

Still, Ma came as soon as she heard I was in the hospital.

"Hey, Mom," I say quietly. "Thanks."

Her eyes dart up and her body is stiller than I've ever seen it.

"I know I don't always make things easy on you," I say, looking down, "and I don't tell you enough how much I appreciate you. You work so hard to make sure Xander and I can keep doing what we love." I meet her eyes. "I love you, Ma."

Her bottom lip pops out and trembles like a nervous Chihuahua. "Alice," she says and takes my hand. "Maybe I won't ever understand why you love hockey. But I do understand that I love you so much...even with that haircut."

I laugh and pull her close for a hug. "I'm still not sitting in that wheelchair."

Mom relents and we walk down to the lobby. Mom lines

up at the reception desk to complete my discharge papers. "Where's Xander?" I ask.

"He was at the theater for rehearsal. I gave him a call but his phone was off. "

So I don't have to face Xander quite yet. I take in a deep breath. It hurts, but less than earlier, thanks to the drugs I'm on.

"ALICE!"

I turn. Sitting in the lobby, a bag of ice pressed up against his face, is Freddy.

The first thing I do is put the hood up on my fluffy pink coat. In my mind, I begrudgingly thank my mother for this perfect disguise. Next, I walk as far away from Mom as I can. If Freddy mentions anything about Xander playing hockey in front of her, I'm dead.

He gets up and walks over to me. I notice his right hand is bound. Something must have happened after I got knocked down, because I definitely took the worst of that hit. He throws his ice pack down on one of the lobby chairs, revealing a bloody mess of a nose, slanting drastically to one side of his face.

"Alice," he says again, and wraps his arms around me. I go stiff, not just because he's pressing against the ribs he bruised two hours ago, but because being this close to Freddy is like being hugged by a giant rat, with his slimy tail slithering around me. I push away from him.

"You do know we broke up, right?" I growl. Typical Freddy, still trying to make me his property.

He laughs, and runs a hand through his blond curls. I notice the ends have a bit of dried blood on them. "Me and your bro had a little run in today." He shrugs. "How's he doing?"

"Bruised ribs," I hiss. "Xander did that to you?" I point toward his bandaged hand.

"Just a couple dislocated fingers." He sighs and looks off into the distance. I think I know who did it, but I hope I'm wrong. "Falcons have one fucked up captain. Serves him right, though. He's suspended for five games." He laughs and my stomach sinks all the way to the floor. Hayden just got captain! He can't be suspended, not now. The team needs him.

I need him.

"Look, Alice." Freddy steps forward and I take one back to keep the distance between us. "I was gonna call."

I can barely look at him, so I stare at Ma, still at the reception desk. "Freddy," I mumble, "I don't care. I gotta go…"

He grabs my arm. "I'm sure Xander's told you things about me, but they're not true. He doesn't know what he saw."

I feel my arm shaking, like I'm afraid. Afraid of Freddy? No. Afraid of what he's taken away from me. My pride. The trust between my brother and me. Rage simmers in my pained chest and my breath is hot and heavy with this anger.

"Xander was confused. That girl was my—"

"Freddy. Stop." I yank my arm away. "I know you purposely hurt my brother today. I know everything you've said to him. Everything you've said about him."

Freddy takes a step back now.

"I don't care if he's gay or not. It doesn't matter," I say, and I don't care that my voice is so loud, the entire lobby turns to us. "You know what does matter? That damaged hand of yours. You wanna know why?"

He shakes his head, but I go on. "Maybe it will heal. Maybe it won't. Maybe it'll just ache a little every time you hold your stick, or maybe your shot will be just an inch off. But that's a big deal for a mediocre player like you. Maybe now your punches won't be as hard. Maybe the Ice Wolves will realize they don't need a conniving, undermining, asshole like you on their team."

For the first time ever, he's silent.

"Or maybe not." I shrug. "But I know I don't need your conniving, undermining asshole self around me or my brother. Leave us alone and maybe your next trip to Chicago won't be spent in the ER."

He backs away, but hits the lobby chair. I can tell he's trying to think of something to say back to me, but his mind keeps drawing a blank, judging from that stricken look on his face.

A presence comes up from behind me and I feel a hand tighten on my shoulder. "Ready to go, sweetie?"

I turn and smile at Ma. "Yeah."

"Oh hello, Galen!" My mom beams. "So nice to see you again!"

He nods and stutters, "Hi, R-Rosaline."

"Oh Galen, look at you! Your handsome face...ruined!" She puts an arm around me and pulls me close. "It's been a rough night, tonight. Our poor Alice was playing in her women's league and got knocked against the board and bruised her ribs. She told me it even shattered the glass!"

I stop breathing. I can't even move.

Freddy doesn't move either. Not his body anyways. But his eyes come alive, looking me over with a sick understanding.

Mom keeps chattering on about her upcoming Ice Ball, what a cute couple we were, her new charity, but none of it matters. All that matters is the look he's giving me.

I thought I'd won. I thought I'd gotten the best of him.

But Freddy exploits weaknesses like the shark he is, and he's just found blood.

I think my mother says good-bye, because Freddy shakes her hand, then smirks at me. "See you around."

I walk like a statue toward the exit, one stone step at a time, when I hear him call out: "Hey Alice!"

I don't want to turn around, but I do, seeing his pale eyes and blood-smattered face. "Tell Al I'll see him on the ice."

Chapter Sixteen

"A five-game suspension." Kevin draws out each word like its own separate sentence. Like each word is another knife I personally drove into his heart.

I shift uncomfortably on the kitchen chair. The overhead light is fluorescent, making me feel like I'm sitting in an interrogation office.

At the beginning of the night, when Coach Z first handed me the jersey with the C, I thought tonight would be amazing. I'd come home... No, *we'd* come home. Al and I. Best friends who worked hard together for our letters. I'd hold it out for Kevin to see, and he'd...

Well, I don't know what he'd do. I don't even know what I wanted from him.

Not this, that's for fucking sure. Him standing above me, lecturing me, like he's my goddamn father.

But Dad was never like this.

Or maybe he never had to be...

Because *I* was never like this. Not until after the accident.

"Coach Zabinski showed me the replay of that hit, Hayden. What were you thinking, coming up behind him? You're lucky he just hurt his hand. You could have seriously injured him. You know better. I know you do." He runs a hand over his beard, then says more softly, "You did that on purpose. You wanted to hurt him."

My hands tighten on the chair. I don't have anything to say, because, *yes,* I wanted to hurt Fredlund. But I can't tell my brother why.

Kevin turns his back, rests his hand on the edge of the countertop, his knuckle white. I was a fool to think things would be different once we got back from Winnipeg.

"You've been...so different this season. For the better. Zabinski told me you made Captain tonight."

I cross my arms and sink down. "It doesn't matter now."

"You're right, it doesn't," Kevin says, turning around to look at me. "You've left the Falcons without a captain for five games."

I hear the door click open in the hallway, followed by Eleanor's bright voice. "Goood evening, family!" she chimes. "I've brought home Thai food!"

I get up and storm toward my basement suite. I can't see Eleanor, not right now. I can't have the two of them look at me, the black spot in their happy family.

I collapse on my ice-cold bed and grab my phone.

Seventeen missed calls from "Al". Thirty-two text messages. The last one reads: "I'm outside." That was twenty minutes ago. Why would she be here?

Slowly, I get up. There's no way she was stupid enough to wait around in the cold. I open my door and look down to see a neon pink heap curled on my stoop.

She's waiting for me.

. . .

ALICE

The door finally opens. I jump up, heart lurching into gear, then casually try to brush the snow off my jacket so he doesn't realize how long I've been sitting out here. "Why didn't you answer your phone?"

He takes a moment to answer, and I realize he's taking me in, like the witness of an accident. With sudden horror, I realize I'm still wearing the pink jacket with faux fur that Mom brought for me at the hospital. I cross my arms, trying to hide as much of the monstrosity as I can.

My thoughts run rampant as I wait for his silent judgement to end. I know I should be at home resting—and waiting for these painkillers to wear off—but instead I snuck out and drove here. I have to make sure everything is still...

Still what? The same? Because it's not. And I know it never will be again.

Finally, he meets my gaze. "What are you doing here?"

"I, uh..." I swallow, my voice hoarse from the cold, dry air. "I thought we should talk about...this."

"I told you before. I won't tell anyone your secret. Is there anything else?"

I bite my lip. Well, that pretty much sums it up. I needed to know he won't tell Coach or any of the other players... and I believe him. Yet I stand here fidgeting, while my heart hammers against my sore rib cage.

Finally, when I can't bare the silence anymore, I say: "Uh, no. That's it."

He begins to shut the door. "Okay. Bye."

My stomach feels heavy. I tilt back my head and groan. "Hayden...look, I'm sorry, okay?"

He pushes the door a bit more closed. "Yeah, okay. See

you."

I throw my hand forward, stopping the door. Dark circles rim his eyes, and he's pale as the ice. "Are...are we okay?"

He doesn't release his pressure on the door, and I find myself pushing hard to keep it open. "Are we okay?" he repeats.

"Like friends?"

He laughs, but there's no joy in it. "Friends?" He spits out the word, as if the sound of it is toxic. "I don't even know you."

"B-but," I stammer.

He puts his face right against the crack in the door. Golden light trickles out around him, but it makes his face completely black. "Al was my best friend. I shared things with Al I've never shared with anyone. He was my friend because of our conversations, our memories. I valued his humor. His honesty. You have none of those things. You, *Alice* Bell, are a stranger to me."

My body trembles. I want to tell him that he's wrong. That it was me—the real me—all those times. Everything I said to him, everything we did, was real. But how can I even know that's the truth, when all of it was messed up in a tangled lie?

He stares down, cast in shadow, and waits for me to speak.

But I've never been very good with words. There's only one way to show him all of this was real, that despite the lies, my feelings are true. I push against the door, grab his neck, and kiss him.

At first, he does nothing. His body is rigid and straight, and his mouth cold beneath mine. Then he moves. His hands start in my hair, tangling around the back of my head before drifting down my neck to the small of my back. I gasp as he brushes against my ribs, but he steals my breath in a kiss.

I push into him, losing myself in his touch. His lips are crushing, hungry for mine, and I lace my fingers through his curly hair.

Then, in an instant, he pulls away. I lean against the doorframe, my vision spinning. His face is curled in disgust.

Hayden shakes his head and wipes his mouth. "You're manipulative, Alice Bell, and I'm tired of being your pawn. Leave."

The shadows and light swirl together as my eyes fill with tears. I want to yell at him. To push him. To tell him he doesn't understand. But none of it will do any good. I don't feel like a hockey player. Or a good sister. Or anything at all. I just feel like a girl who got her heart broken.

Chapter Seventeen

ALICE

The mascara Madison made me put on runs down my face. The whole audience is in stitches. Even though each bout of laughter makes my bruised ribs ache, I can't stop howling.

Mom turns to me. "I don't get it." At least she's trying.

Xander's play was an absolute hit. When he comes out to take his bow, the audience rises to their feet, hooting and hollering. How could I not have realized he was the lead? All these months, I was so concerned about my acting, I didn't even think once about his.

The roar of the crowd, the smiling faces of the troupe... it's almost like hockey. And as Xander bows low, a humble smile across his face, I realize this is his Stanley Cup.

· · ·

Much later, after countless good-byes where I stood awkwardly to the side, Xander and I make it to the car. Mom left earlier to dash off to her last minute charity meeting.

With the Ice Ball two days away, she's been running around like a chicken with its head cut off.

And if the ball is two days away, that means tomorrow is my first game back from my injury. And Hayden's first game back from his suspension. The Falcons have lost every game since we've been away. Thinking of it makes me feel as if there's a heavy shroud over my shoulders. I shrug off the thought.

Xander trills the car ride away, talking about funny backstage moments and mistakes the cast made (of course, no one else could pick up on them). When we pull into our driveway, I turn off the car but don't move to go in. As much as I'd love to crawl upstairs and pretend tomorrow is never going to happen, I know I have to sort things out with my brother. For the last few weeks, we've been pretending everything is fine and our fight never happened. But it's time for me to do something I never thought I'd have the courage to do.

"Xander," I say, "can we talk?"

"Alice wants to talk?" Xander laughs. "What, is the world ending and no one wanted to tell me?"

I drop my hands from their vice grip on the steering wheel. "Ugh, forget it!"

He touches my hand, and I look at him. He's smiling, as if he's still glowing from the light of the play. If there was ever a good moment to talk about something, it would be now.

I take a deep breath.

"I know you're gay." I didn't plan out anything eloquent or beautiful to say, but it seems dumb to just leave it there, so I stammer on. "Freddy told me. But I want you to know it doesn't matter to me, not even a little. I love you no matter what. You're my best friend."

Xander sits back in his seat, and I can hear his heavy breath in the dark car. The silence sits like a third passenger.

"I guess I needed to tell you eventually," he finally says.

"God knows, you would never have realized it on your own."

"What's that supposed to mean?"

"Only that you're the most oblivious person on the planet." Xander laughs. "Come on, Al, you thought hockey was America's national sport until last year!"

"Hmm." I stroke my chin. "Good point. But I'm only the second most oblivious person on the planet."

He smiles, and we say it together: "Next to Mom."

And it's not even funny, but we break out giggling, filling the car with our identical laugh.

When we're gasping for breath and wiping tears from our eyes, I take Xander's hand. "I'm sorry. You were right this whole time. I was so selfish, and I wasn't there when you needed me most."

He runs a hand through his hair. "I lied to you too, Al. I kept Freddy's secret to protect my own. We've both been selfish."

A small smile creeps up my face. "Soo…can we just agree we both suck?"

He gives me an identical smile back. "Worst twins on the planet."

I pull him into a hug. "Do we get to talk about hot guys together now?"

"I'm pretty sure there's only one hot guy you want to talk about."

Hayden and I have had to go and watch the Falcons lose, game after game. Not once has he said anything to me, or even looked at me at all. I never thought I could make anyone hate me the way he does. "That…that doesn't matter. Not anymore." I look at Xander out of the corner of my eye. "You think he's hot, too?"

Xander turns serious. "What do you mean, it doesn't matter?"

I fidget with the volume knob, gathering my courage

to tell him about the next part of the story. "Hayden found out." Before he can interrupt, I tell him everything from the bonfire, to the hotel room, to Christmas, to the moment he walked in on me in the trainer's office.

He doesn't say anything when I'm done. "I'm sorry, Xander. I'm so sorry. I'm not going to go to the game tomorrow…or go back ever. I'll tell Coach I'm too injured to play until your leg is strong enough—"

"I don't want that."

"What?"

"I don't want to play hockey again," he says flatly.

"But you've been playing hockey your whole life!"

"Exactly!" he says, laughing a little. "This was the first year I've actually felt like I could breathe! That I could actually focus on my acting because I wasn't trying so hard to be a hockey player. This was the first year that I could be, well, me."

I try to wrap my head around this. Hockey has been everything to me and Xander since we could walk.

Or maybe it's just been everything to me, and I was too oblivious to realize it.

"Don't you miss it?" I ask.

"Parts of it, I guess," he says. "But we both know I wouldn't have made the Falcons if it wasn't for you. And at this level, it's all-or-nothing. And I would have had to give everything I am to even scrape by on the 4th line. I was prepared and willing to do it, because I wanted so bad to be someone I'm not." He runs a hand over his face. "But maybe breaking my leg made me selfish, because I don't think I'm willing to give up that part of myself anymore."

"You need to do what makes you happy," I say. "Are you gonna tell people?"

"Yeah," he says quietly. "Not right away, though. One at a time. Mom first."

"Ma will understand. I mean, if she can get over me cutting off my hair, then she'll get over anything!"

"True enough." He laughs. Then he reaches up and turns on the little light in the car, so that I can really see his face. "So, Al, if you do go back tomorrow, I want you to go back for you. You love that team with everything you are. Just do what Alice Bell wants to do."

I close my eyes and think. "How am I supposed to do what Alice Bell wants, when I don't even know who she is?" I flash Xander a look, but he's silent. "Now would be a good time for one of your insightful quotes."

He gives a wry smile. "How the hell is anyone, except yourself, going to tell you who you are?"

"But I don't know."

"Stop trying to be a different person for all these different people. Just…play your game."

I mull it over as we leave the car and walk into our house. As I step into my bedroom alone, I wonder about all the different versions of myself. Alice the daughter, the sister, the girlfriend, the figure skater. And Al, the hockey player. The rookie. The friend.

Maybe none of these are lies. All of them make up the mosaic of my life, a picture of broken glass and scars. But there's beauty there, too.

All I know is, I am a girl who loves her family. And hockey is more than a game to me. It's part of me.

I walk to my closet and pick up my jersey. Number forty-four. We've come far this season, and the playoffs are so close, I can taste them. I've been the one sweating and hurting and testing myself to get this team to where we are.

And I won't stop now.

• • •

HAYDEN

There's no way I'm nervous. I haven't been nervous before a game...well, ever. *So why am I sitting in my goddamn Jeep?* My fists clench and unclench on the steering wheel. I've watched my whole team walk into the arena.

I'm the captain now, and I've left my team alone for the last five games. And they lost all five of them.

Now, we're about to play our biggest rivals: the Ice Wolves. And if we don't win this game, we won't have enough points to make it into the playoffs.

Despite the chill, sweat drips down my brow. I'm the captain. I should have been the first one in, prepared with a rousing speech to motivate my team. Outside the clouds break open, and rain *rat-tat-tats* on my roof.

Where is she? I search the parking lot for the eight millionth time. No sign of her old sedan. Alice was out five games, same as me, and now it looks like she's not even going to show up. Anger grows in me again. If she hadn't gotten hit...

Your emotions got the best of you, Hayden. My brother's voice plays in my head. *And those losses? That's on you, Captain.*

I smack the dashboard with my fist. It's not fair! Kevin doesn't know what he's talking about. He doesn't know what Alice did to me.

There are going to be NHL scouts watching the playoff games. How do you plan to get noticed if you're not in the playoffs, Captain?

My sweat drips cold, and I force Kevin's voice out of my head.

A bus pulls up in front of the arena, and the Ice Wolves file out. I scan their faces, looking for Fred. I guess I'm lucky I didn't hit him hard enough to put him out for too long, otherwise I could have been suspended for the rest of the season. But I'll have to be careful: he'll be gunning for me tonight.

A ratty red car skids over the wet roads and parks shoddily. A sickening spurt of adrenaline surges through my gut. *She's here, she's here, she's here.*

I whack my forehead. Why do I give a shit? Now it's just going to be excruciatingly awkward. Yet, my heart sprints in my chest, and I hurriedly snatch my gear from the passenger's seat.

She's dressed exactly how I remember: wearing her gear already like a total loser. The rain plasters her hair across her face. Of course she's not using an umbrella. That's just not something Al would do.

One of the Ice Wolves breaks away from the pack as the rest of the team heads inside. He saunters toward Alice.

Fredlund.

My body stiffens. I need to ignore them and just head into the arena. But instead, I jump out of the Jeep and head toward them.

The image of Fred decking Alice flashes across my mind. Her grimace in pain as she sat on the trainer's bench. He wanted to hurt her then, and he could want to hurt her now—

But as I get closer, I notice something is off. The way he's standing over her, the leer on his face. He reaches forward and wraps an arm around her waist.

Ice floods through my body, and I stop. He knows.

Alice couldn't tell me her secret, but she told *him*. She told the fucker who cheated on her, but she couldn't tell *me?*

Alice jerks away from Fred, raising her hockey stick like a sword. Her voice grows loud and menacing.

She's got this under control. I turn to stumble into the arena, but they've both spotted me. Fred huffs and walks toward me. I smile slightly at the crook in his nose. "Looking forward to seeing you on the ice, Captain," he sneers as he brushes past me. Then he turns back and gives a skin-crawling smile to Alice. "You too, Allie."

He disappears into the arena, and I'm left staring at Alice's wide eyes. She looks as if she's about to say something, so I quickly turn and head into the arena.

"Hayden, wait!" She rushes to catch up to me. "It's not like I told him. He saw me in the ER and figured it out."

I push the door but don't hold it open for her. "I believe you. Whatever's in the best interest for Alice, always."

"Be quiet!" She grabs my arm and looks down the empty concrete hallway.

I walk faster, trying to ignore her, but her presence lingers behind me. I wish she hadn't come back. How am I supposed to concentrate on the most important game of the season when I'm worried she's going to get creamed every shift? How am I supposed to trust her to be there in a play when she's spent every day lying to me? And how am I supposed to be a captain and bring my team together when I want her as far out of my life as possible?

I grit my teeth. That's it. Starting now, she doesn't exist to me.

I know how to score goals without Al Bell.

• • •

ALICE

The clock ticks down to zero as the second period ends. I feel my whole team rise up around me with a pathetic moan. 2–0 for the Ice Wolves. I've never felt so low in my life. How could I have thought that everything would be normal again once I came back?

First, Freddy taunting me as I walked into the arena. I know he won't reveal my secret tonight: he stashes secrets like a rat. But every time I see him, it'll be like he's holding a loaded gun, ready to fire.

And what did I expect it to be like on the ice? That Hayden and I would have the same chemistry we usually do? No, he's gone back to his favorite move of not passing to me. I can't even be mad. I deserve all of this.

But the Falcons don't. This is our last chance at the playoffs...and we're failing. Because of me.

I'm the last one on the bench. All this time I had been lying to myself, pretending I was here so I could help Xander. No, I was playing because I loved it. Because I wanted to prove I could outplay those who didn't believe in me. And I told Hayden I lied to him to protect Xander's secret. But that was a lie, too. I was too afraid to lose everything I had built. Not just my place on the team, but what we shared.

How ironic.

I shake my head. None of it matters now. I have to stop thinking about me. It's time to put the Falcons first.

I jump up and follow my team. They sulk around the locker room, silent and sullen. Coach resembles a bomb, red-faced and ready to pop.

"You get soft on your days off, Bell?" Coach snaps. "Pick it up next period."

My cheeks redden. Maybe I could, if someone actually passed me the puck! *That's thinking about you, Alice.* I can't do that anymore.

I walk over to Hayden. He purposefully looks in the other direction.

"I need to talk to you," I say, low enough that no one else can hear.

He yawns.

"Fine, don't talk," I say through gritted teeth. "Just listen. I want to offer you a deal."

"A deal?" He gives a cruel laugh. "This should be

interesting."

At least I got a reaction out of him. I turn and to my surprise, he follows me. We enter the trainer's office. Suddenly, I feel very hot and take off my helmet.

"So?" he says, leaning on the door, as if he's afraid to come too far into the room with me.

I swallow, my throat dry. How can I put my thoughts into words he will understand? "I know I can't ever make it right between us. What I did was wrong, and I don't blame you for hating me." The words sit like a pile of stones on my tongue. I can count on one hand the times I've admitted I'm wrong. I force myself to meet his dark gaze and continue.

"But maybe I can make things right by the team." I cross my arms. "If we win tonight, the Falcons start the playoffs in a couple weeks."

Hayden paces in the doorway. "Did you bring me in here to tell me what's at stake? I already know! Everyone has been drilling it into me. If I screw up two seasons in a row, I can kiss my chances of being drafted good-bye. I goddamn know what's at stake!"

"I won't come back!" I shout back at him. His body stills. "That's what I'm trying to say. After this game, I'll quit the Falcons for good."

"What do you mean?" He fully steps inside the room.

"Look…I know you don't want to play with me anymore. But if we work together tonight, we might be able to …no, I *know* we can catch up. We can win! You just have to play with me one last time. Then you'll never have to see me again."

"Why would you do that?" He stares at me intently. "There's nothing in the world you love more than hockey."

"That was before I met…uh…I-I was never supposed to be here, anyways. I'm never going to play in the NHL. It's time to do something right." I have to turn away from him. This is bigger than me. Even bigger than the Falcons.

This is for Hayden.

If we lose tonight and don't make it to the playoffs, he won't get noticed by the NHL scouts and show them the captain he's become. My stomach twists inside as I think about him living without his dream.

Those stupid tears spring to my eyes again. He may be short-tempered and wear dumb hats and lose himself to his emotions…but he's the kindest person I've ever known. Those emotions that rule him—they rule me, too. I could get lost in his smile or drown myself in his sorrow. And after all he's been through…he needs a little happiness.

My voice cracks as I struggle to talk. "Look, I can deal with you hating me, but I can't watch you lose everything you've worked so hard for. Don't pass to me for me—do it for the Falcons. We don't have to be best friends: you can be the captain of the Falcons, and I'll just be a player who can help this team win. That's it. It doesn't mean you forgive me. But right now, like it or not, I'm your team's best chance to win this game."

He stands like a statue and the only sound is the clock ticking away. Then he turns and begins to leave.

"Hayden?" I say. "Do we have a deal?"

He doesn't look back as he says: "Coach has us on a line together for a reason. Let's remind everyone why."

. . .

The moment we step onto the ice, I immediately know that Hayden's agreed to my deal. I've somehow managed to shift his view of me from liar to teammate—at least for the next twenty minutes.

He wins the faceoff, and I land his first pass right away. Our practiced plays come to life on the ice, and the Wolves can't keep up with us. I know exactly where Hayden will be when I fake a shot but pass to him. He one-times it into the net, and that sweet red light bursts to life.

The arena explodes, but it's all white noise to me. There's nothing but Hayden and me. Every shift feels like clockwork, seamless and in tune. I fly on my skates, and it's like we can read the other's mind.

This is how it's supposed to be.

Hayden fires me a pass, and I stickhandle straight through three of the Ice Wolves before I reach the net. Bam! Goal number two...a tie game! The Falcons surround me cheering. I catch Hayden's eye, and I know he's feeling it, too. This heated connection between us.

My heart hammers in my chest, and I look away. Now is no time to be lovesick. We're one goal away from the playoffs. My stomach sinks as I head to the bench. I have to savor this: my last game with the Falcons.

The Ice Wolves' coach calls a time-out, and we gather around Coach Z. But instead, Hayden stands up.

All the eyes on the bench turn to him. He's red-faced, sweaty, exhausted. We all look the same. And victory is just as close as defeat.

"Can anyone tell me," Hayden says, his voice growing louder with each word, "how many years it's been since the Falcons have made the playoffs?"

"Five," Tyler says quietly.

"Five years," Hayden says. "And one game can change all that." He skates in front of the bench, going up and down the line like a general in front of his troops. "One game. One goal. I've let you down. As your captain and as your teammate, I've let you down." His jaw stiffens. "But no more. I'm playing for the bird on the front." He smacks his jersey. "And not the name on the back." He narrows his eyes. "And I'm playing for all of you. Every single one of us was meant to be here." His eyes flick over me. "And Falcons stay together."

Slowly, the team rises, and Hayden throws his stick up in the air. "Who are we?"

"FALCONS!" the team roars, thrusting their sticks up too.

"Who are we playing for?"

"FALCONS!" they roar again.

"WHO ARE WE?" Hayden yells.

This time, I can't help myself. I throw my stick up too and shout with the team: "FALCONS!"

"Come on, boys," Hayden says as the buzzer blows. "Let's soar."

Coach grunts his approval and smacks me on the back. "Glad to see to you've finally got your skates laced up straight. Tremblay and Bell, finish this off."

There's only two minutes before the end of the period. We need a goal. Hayden looks over at me as we line up. "Stay with me, Bell."

I nod, and the puck drops. The Ice Wolves have put Freddy out against us. Suddenly, my ribs ache as if they remember what he did to me. I don't want to get anywhere near him.

But Freddy wins the faceoff. He skates toward our end. As he sprints past me, he looks up, flashing me his slimy grin.

It's a lesson I taught Hayden at our very first practice, and I'll teach it to Freddy now.

Never take your eyes off the puck.

I dart in front of him, sneaking my stick around his and snatching the puck. Breath comes ragged in my throat as I hightail it toward the net. Behind me, Freddy screams with frustration. There's only one person between me and the net.

I pass the puck to Hayden, and he shoots it in.

Goal!

A flood of blue surrounds me, but I push my way to Hayden. With only thirty seconds to go in the game, victory is right in front of us. And I don't care if he hates me—we did it. Together.

I force myself right under his nose. "How'd you get such a clean goal like that, Tremblay?"

He smiles at me, a real smile that reaches his deep brown eyes. Despite our team and the roaring crowd, it feels like we're the only two people in the world. And everything is okay.

"Had help from some short rookie." He puts his hand on my helmet.

We skate back to the bench, but we're blocked by a large, looming figure. Freddy stands in front of us.

"What did you do to Captain Tremblay to get him to favor you on the ice, Allie?" Freddy spits. "Probably everything you were too much of a stuck-up bitch to do with me."

I stop skating. "Uh, what?"

His brows creep up his face. "You heard me, Alice. I see now how you got so good."

Hayden tightens his grip on his stick. "Al's always been better than you."

Freddy's ice-chip eyes burrow into Hayden like daggers, and he drops his gloves. "Bring it, Tremblay."

Hayden stands there, jaw tense, but he doesn't move. My heart hammers in my chest; Hayden can't get in another fight, not now.

Freddy throws his head back and laughs. "Too afraid to face me, Captain? Playing with a girl's made you soft!"

"You want to see how soft this girl is?" I throw my gloves off. Anger courses through my blood.

Freddy raises an eyebrow and starts to laugh. I don't let him get a single smarmy sound out before I surge forward and snatch his jersey. He tries to knock me away, but I hold my ground.

I told myself it didn't hurt when he cheated on me. But it

did. It fucking hurt—and I want to make him hurt too. I pry his helmet off. It clangs to the ice, and I can see his face: all sweaty and red and veiny—nothing attractive about that now.

Freddy didn't get to be the goon for years without having taken some hits himself...like the rib he broke ten months ago.

Maybe it's a low blow, but so is cheating on me. So is blackmailing my brother. So is checking me into the boards so hard it broke the glass.

I wind my fist back, and hit him in the rib with all the hatred I can muster.

He squeals like a stuck pig and clutches his stomach. Hot madness runs through me and I don't stop. I curl up my fist the way Hayden taught me so long ago and punch him straight in the nose. He falls back, blood gushing from his fingers.

"I'd suggest you keep what you know to yourself, Fred," I say, lowering my voice, "unless you want everyone in the league to know you got your ass kicked by a girl."

He looks up at me glaring, his nose broken for the second time in a month.

Sorry, handsome.

The ref slings an arm around me and skates me toward the penalty bench. It might as well be a golden throne. I turn around to see Freddy's crying face one last time.

Instead, I catch Hayden's eye. He grins at me—and my heart sails right out of my chest. Instead of forcing it away, I let it float inside me. This is my last game playing for the Falcons, playing with Hayden. Even with everything I've done, I think I can be happy for the next thirty seconds.

· · ·

HAYDEN

With Fredlund's complete annihilation, the Ice Wolves barely give a yip for the last thirty seconds.

The clock runs out, and the game ends. Three to two for the Falcons.

The crowd erupts so loudly, I think the whole arena might explode. The team jumps off the bench screaming as if we've just won the Stanley Cup. Coach Z holds my gaze and gives me a proud nod. My body flushes with relief. For the first time in five years, the Falcons are going to the playoffs.

It really is all because of Alice. I'm pretty sure she can do anything if she puts her mind to it.

The team surrounds Al and me. We actually pulled it off…not just the deal we made before third period, but the one we made months ago. She said she'd help me make it to the playoffs, and I said I'd teach her to fight. Looks like we both succeeded.

Before I look down, I can tell she's in front of me. The connection we had on the ice is still palpable even now. She's being crushed between our goalie and Sacs in a huge hug—but as if she can sense my gaze, she turns her face toward mine. It's impossible not to see her as a girl now; with her big doe eyes, and round face. How did I not notice how beautiful she was before?

And this last period…it was like nothing had ever changed between us. On the ice, she was my teammate. But here—I find myself lost in those giant gray eyes again—she's *Alice*. Whoever that is to me.

The team disbands back to the locker room to celebrate, until it's just me and her on the ice. She looks over at me almost shyly. I guess she thinks I hate her.

Which I do.

But with the high of the win, it's hard to feel any of that right now. "Good punch," I murmur.

"Thanks," she says, and then skates back a little bit. "I'm really gonna miss this."

There's no resentment or hatred in her voice. Only sadness. She looks around the arena, as if soaking it in, with her mouth guard half-hanging out of her mouth. It always bugs me how she does that.

I skate closer to her and gently push her mouth guard back into place. "You'll have to stop doing that," I say, "unless you want to lose some teeth in the playoffs."

She's silent, and I realize I still have my thumb on her lip. I quickly drop my hand.

"The playoffs," she breathes, looking up at me. "Seriously?"

"You're the best line mate I've had. That's the truth," I say. "I don't want you to give up hockey. The Falcons need Al Bell in the playoffs."

"Right. The Falcons need me," she murmurs, skating toward the bench. She gives me a weak smile. "Well, tell Captain Tremblay that #44 will be there!"

I stand still for a moment, not quite ready to leave the ice. The crowd's clearing out, and all the players are in the locker room. I just told Alice I didn't want her to quit. I thought she'd be excited, but instead, a cloud of sadness still hangs above her.

"I-I'll…see you in the locker room?" she says and steps off the ice.

"Yeah, I'll be there in a minute."

When she's gone, I take a deep breath and do a full lap around the rink. I can't think about Alice anymore. Whatever we have on the ice doesn't matter—she still lied to me.

Just as I'm about to head in, I spot the puck, still in the net. I bend over and pick it up. A memento, from the game where all our dreams came true.

Chapter Eighteen

HAYDEN

I lie on my couch, tossing the puck up and down above my head. Even though the game was last night, a million thoughts still threaten to break out of my brain. It takes effort to turn my head when Kevin lumbers down the stairs. He stands at the entryway, smiling.

"Pretty good game last night, Hayden," he says. "Eleanor and I were able to make it for the last period."

"That was the only good part of the game," I mumble. I had been able to avoid Kevin and Eleanor after the game, but I knew I would have to face him today.

Kevin sits down on the arm of the couch. "It can take a while to get back into it after an absence. From what I saw, your team is one hundred percent with you, and you're one hundred percent with them. That's what's important."

I give an inward smile. That last period had felt right, like everything had finally come together.

"I'm not supposed to mention anything," Kevin says, a

grin bursting through his bushy beard, "but as the captain of the number one NHL team in the Central Division, I do tend to hear a thing or two about scouting and potential..."

I jerk up. "What?!"

"Our scouts were watching you play last night. The higher ups were very impressed."

A smile threatens to tear my face in half. "Are you serious?"

"I'm serious," Kevin says. "You'll still need to wait a year to get drafted...but just keep doing what you're doing. If you play like this next year, there's no telling how far you could go."

"Hey now," I say laughing, "if it's true, I might be stuck with you in Chicago for the rest of my life!"

Kevin crinkles his eyes. "Would that really be so bad?"

"I guess not," I murmur. It would be pretty cool to be around as my new niece or nephew grows up.

Kevin stands and claps a hand on my shoulder. "So we're thinking of leaving in about ten minutes. You want to ride with us?"

"For what?"

"The charity Ice Ball at the arena. The Falcons are scheduled to make an appearance. I know Zabinski's insisting the whole team be there."

My stomach feels heavy, like I just ate an entire plate of Sacachelli's homemade spaghetti. That damned charity ball. My grip tightens on the puck in my lap. "I'm not going."

Kevin looks at me quizzically, but he doesn't break into a lecture about how it's my duty as captain to attend. Instead, his face softens. "Hayden...where's Al?"

I plop back on the couch, turning my back to him. "The ball."

"All right." Kevin walks to the door. But because he's Kevin, he turns back and says: "In our whole life, I've never seen you bond with anyone the way you did with Al. I'd hate to see you give that up...because of what? A fight? Because you're both stubborn?" He shakes his head. "Think of how many times we've fought and made up. What would have happened if one of us had just given up?"

I wish I could tell Kevin the whole story, but a part of me wonders if he already knows. And another part of me keeps asking myself why I'm so mad. What does it mean to me now that Alice is a girl? She was still the same #44 on the ice today. So why is she different off the ice?

She waited outside my house the night I found out she was a girl. And she kissed me like she meant it. My body reacted before my mind had a chance to catch up: kissing her back, my hands on her neck. But that's how it's always been with Al, ever since I met her: instinctual, as if I'm the puck, and she's the stick, guiding me to her every whim.

But she lied. Even when I shared the darkest parts of my life with her, her light was still a lie.

And this terrible feeling keeps knotting itself in my chest over and over again. Because I know why that lie hurts so much.

Al is so much more than a teammate to me. She's even more than a friend.

I'm in love with her.

"I really hope you decide to come, Hayden," Kevin says as he heads upstairs. "One bad period doesn't equal a bad game."

• • •

I stay on the couch until I hear the car pull out of the driveway. The puck lies on my chest. I can't go to the ball. I can't talk to her, but I'm pretty sure trying to ignore her would be like trying to ignore a million sirens going off at once.

The doorbell rings from upstairs. That's weird. I have no idea who would be visiting at this hour, and I didn't order any food. I shove the puck in my pocket and head upstairs.

When I open the door, my pulse roars in my ears.

It's Al.

I blink. Wait, it's not Al. It's like a shadow of Al, wearing her same baggy hoodie and jeans. The eyes are the same cloudy gray, but they don't shine quite like Al's do. And the mouth is all wrong: a straight line instead of the exaggerated frown.

"Hi," the shadow says, "I'm Xander. I'm Alice's—"

"Brother," I breathe.

He raises an eyebrow at me. "Can I, uh, come in?"

I step back and let him walk in.

He stands in the hallway. Christ, I've never met him before but even the way he stands is familiar, rocking on the balls of his feet. "I need to talk to you about Al," he says.

"Okay." I cross my arms and hear the defensiveness in my voice. "What?"

He throws his hands out beside him and shrugs. "Look, I get what she did—what we did—was wrong. But she kept my secret because we're family. You have a brother, right? Wouldn't you do anything for family?"

"Of course," I say. "Alice and I worked it out today. We can still play hockey together, so it's fine."

"Is it?" Xander says, and he looks up at me as if he can read my mind. The more I look at him, the more I can see the differences between the two of them. Maybe I'm imagining it, or maybe I've just spent so long looking at her face that I can picture every detail.

I shrug. "I'm not sure what you want me to say."

"I know my sister better than anyone," he says. "She's different...in a good way. I got so mad at her. I told her not to get close to you. But she couldn't help herself. Hockey was

Alice's whole world, until it wasn't." He runs a hand through his hair. "She's my sister, and I owe her for messing with her love life in the wrong way. So that's why I'm here. To make it right. To see if you felt the same and were just being as stubborn as she is."

All of his words circle around my head, scrambling my thoughts. I step back until I run into the wall. "Felt the same?"

Xander sighs dramatically. "Alice was willing to give up hockey for you." I must give him a blank look because he sighs again. "Tremblay, she's in love with you."

· · ·

ALICE

"You look lovely, sweetheart." Ma straightens the tiara in my hair, and then tilts her head sideways. "I suppose this haircut can look cute at some angles."

I laugh. "Thanks, Mom." I look down at my sparkly electric blue dress, embroidered with white beads: the colors of the Falcons' jersey. I do look cute today.

I walk to the edge of the ice. Despite the packed arena, I feel a brisk chill without all my gear on. Harmony finishes her routine, and everyone in the crowd throws down flowers and teddy bears. Man, is it ever full in here. Mom did an amazing job marketing this thing.

My routine is last, and after that, the Family Fun Skate will begin. The Chicago Falcons and the NHL team are going to join all the families on the ice.

I wonder if Hayden will come. My hand trembles to my lip—the last place he touched me. But I can only think of him as my teammate now. A wave of sadness hits me, but I push it away. At least I still get to play hockey.

Mom pushes me forward as soon as the ice is cleared, and I skate to the middle of the rink. I used to feel out of place every time I figure skated: naked in a short dress and tights instead of my jersey and pads. But as I look around the booming arena, excitement grows through me. I've worked hard for this, too.

The music starts, and I fall into the dance, just as I do when the whistle blows. This is a play, and I know exactly how it's going to go. I land my spin and the crowd claps. I bask in the warmth of their attention.

I fly through the rest of my routine, gliding into the finale with my arms up and a smile on my face.

Maybe I'm a sweatpants-wearing, whole-pizza-eating hockey player. And maybe I'm also a lipstick-wearing, sparkly dress-twirling figure skater. Maybe I'm both of these things mashed together; a work-in-progress, a half-played game.

And maybe Alice and Al aren't so different after all.

Chapter Nineteen

Hayden

I'm panting like crazy by the time Xander and I cut through the locker room and make it out to the bench. As if I wasn't already out of breath, the air is kicked out of me again.

Alice twirls on the ice, a spectacle of blue sparkles and long legs. Damn, those legs. Watching her move on the ice now, it's no wonder she was able to outskate and out-stickhandle every boy on the ice. Her movements are as fluid as water.

I force myself to take a deep breath. I'm not here to ogle her—although if this goes well, I'll have time for that later.

A nervous jolt hits me. I haven't been the nicest person to her lately. Like always, I decided to run instead of facing the music when I needed to. Another lesson learned from Al:

It's time to man up.

"Okay, then go do it," Xander says exasperatedly.

"Did I say all that out loud?"

"You were muttering to yourself. Kind of creepy. Okay,

loverboy, it's game time!" He whacks me on my back.

Her song ends, and she stands in the middle of the rink, looking up into the crowd. A smile so infectious plays across her face and spreads to mine. The arena feels like it's erupting with the crowd's cheers. Stuffed animals and flowers litter the ice.

My throat feels dry, and suddenly I'm afraid to move. "She might not want anything to do with me now."

Xander raises a brow. "You miss one hundred percent of the shots you don't take."

I give a little smile. "Thanks, Gretzky." My grip tightens on the puck. I've taken thousands of shots in my career, but none of them are as important as this one.

This is for you, Al. I toss the game-winning puck onto the ice. It slides along, straight through the flowers and teddy bears, and bumps Alice's skate. She bends down, picks it up, then looks at me.

· · ·

ALICE

I pick up the puck and look across the ice. There, on the bench where I've seen him so many times before, is Hayden Tremblay. He's not wearing the Falcons jersey like the rest of the team, just his plaid shirt and jeans—but he's got skates on. Just when I think things can't get any weirder, I notice my brother standing beside him. I try to catch Xander's eye, but he's not looking at me. Instead, he pushes Hayden forward.

Hayden trips onto the ice, strangely awkward, but keeps heading toward me. I skate back, as if that could keep him from reaching me, and look around. Most of the people in the stands are milling about, preparing to come down for the Fun Skate. However, Hayden's presence draws a few stares. People are probably wondering what he's doing. Hell, I'm wondering what he's doing.

He stops in front of me. His brown curly hair is a mess, falling around his face, and his cheeks are flushed and red. But his brown eyes shine at me, all the lights from the arena reflecting in them. "Alice."

"What?"

"We won the game because of you." He nods toward the puck in my hands, which I've currently got a vice grip on. "You deserve it."

I think back to our first game together. I tried to give him the puck from that game. I look down at it and wonder just how petty it would be if I chucked it across the ice like he did. "A kind gesture to your teammate."

Suddenly, his hand is on my face, and he tilts my chin up so I'm forced to look at him.

"Yes," he says, and his voice is low and rough. "You're my teammate. And my best friend."

"Hayden…" I know I should skate away and take this off the ice, but I can't find the will to move from his touch.

"And you know what else, Alice? You're my conscience, my sounding board, my competitor." He tilts his head back and crinkles his eyes. "And I am desperately in love with you."

I don't have any words, but I have a smile that lights up my whole body.

"I'm in love with you, Al," Hayden says. "You know my heart in ways no one else ever has. You make me a stronger person. A better person. But most of all, a happier person. And I swear, from now on, I will do right by you." He laces his fingers through my hair and leans down, tenderly placing his mouth over mine. The kiss is soft as rain, and although we've done this before, it feels like the first time. And it is the first time he's kissing the real me.

Even though my heart pounds, for once the words don't

get stuck. "I love you, too." I cover his hands with mine. "I'm sorry about everything. I wish I could go back and change it."

"I don't," he says, nuzzling my nose with his.

"You don't?"

"I don't think I would have been able to tell Alice everything I told Al." He grins and his gaze runs over me. "Especially if you were distracting me all the time in sparkly dresses like this one."

"Hey!" I laugh and grab his chin. "I don't look like this all the time, y'know."

"I know." He smiles, still gazing at me. "I just really want to kiss you again."

I float my lips over his. "I wanted to kiss you first."

His hands fly lightning fast to my waist, pulling me against him as he kisses me hard on the mouth. We twirl with the momentum, and a few hoots and hollers spring out from our onlookers. Hayden pulls away and rests his lips on my ear. "You'll have to be faster than that, Bell."

"Is this how's it's going to be from now on?" I give him a little shove. "Everything a competition?"

"That's okay with me, because I know there's something I'll always win at," he says, pulling me tighter. I feel so small, wrapped in his arms and pressed against his hard chest.

"What's that?" I whisper.

"Loving you most."

I pull back and wrap my arms around his neck. I give myself all the time in the world to look at him, with no fear of having to hide my true self. "That's what you think, Captain."

Epilogue

ALICE

I lie back on the picnic blanket, letting the summer sun and smell of grilling meat waft over me.

"Alice, cheese on your burger?" Kevin calls from the BBQ.

"Duh!" I respond.

"Shove over." Hayden plops down beside me on the blanket and pulls up me so my head rests in his lap. I look up into his dark brown eyes, the lazy smile, the little bit of stubble that's started to grow on his jaw.

I never would have believed it if one year ago, someone had told me I would be having a barbeque in Kevin Tremblay's backyard, cuddled in the arms of the captain of the Chicago Falcons—who also happens to be my boyfriend.

Eleanor waddles out of the kitchen, somehow looking better at eight months pregnant than I look after a single slice of pizza. Xander and Madison follow her, carrying an array of salad dishes and fruit to the outdoor table.

A smile sneaks across my face. It feels so good to be out here, lying in the soft grass, with the blue sky above me. Sure, it's not ice or cheering crowds, but I can definitely enjoy this for the summer. Although there's a feeling like an unscratchable itch brewing beneath my skin. I still have to finish what we started.

The Falcons made it to the third round of playoffs before the Cedar Rapid Cougars eliminated us in triple overtime. I would rather be hit by a bus, ran over by said bus, and eaten alive by crows than go through a loss like that again.

And even though it was terrible, I can't help but feel proud, too. The Falcons made the playoffs for the first time in five years! And we'll be even better next year.

Well, maybe. A nervous pang hits my chest, but I fake a smile as Madison and Xander sit down beside us on the picnic blanket. Xander holds my gaze and narrows his eyes. Mind-meld.

"Get out of your head, Bell," he says. "Worry about that tomorrow. Tonight, we're having fun."

Tomorrow is a big day for both Xander and me. He's going to tell Ma he's gay. I know he's nervous, but he hides it well, unlike me.

I'm coming out to Coach Zabinski tomorrow. I'm going to tell him the truth about Al Bell, from start to finish. In an ideal world, he'll apologize for banning me from the team in the first place and see the error of his ways. Worst case, he'll disqualify me from the league.

My phone buzzes, and I sit up to grab my phone off the blanket. Speak of the devil: another text from Coach Z.

Al, how are workouts going? You training hard? Make sure you're eating right. Don't get lazy with your time off! More scouts asking about you for next year's draft! WORK HARD.

"He doesn't ever give you a break, eh?" Hayden says, reading over my shoulder.

"Yeah, well, he knows there's no Tremblay without Bell." I give him a teasing grin and snuggle closer between his legs. He pokes me in the ribs.

I put the phone away without replying. It doesn't matter how many scouts are looking at Al Bell—I'll never play for the NHL. And it's time for Alice to have her turn.

"Here you go," Kevin says in his warm twang and hands me a plate with a burger on it.

"Thanks!" I smile up at him.

Hayden and I told Kevin and Eleanor about my disguise that day after the charity Ice Ball. Kevin never admitted it, but I'm pretty sure he'd figured it out already. I thought they might be mad that I'd lied to them, or cheated my way into playing hockey, but Kevin just told me that I was a damn fine player, either way.

"When you tell Coach Zabinski," Kevin had said, "I'll have your back. You have a right to play for the Falcons, and Coach knows you're why they made it to the playoffs."

At that point, I had zero intention of ever telling Coach Zabinski the truth, but Kevin had other ideas.

"So what, you're just going to keep playing for the Falcons in disguise?"

"Uh. Yeah. That's the plan."

"What about your future?" Kevin had roared, and I suddenly had a very clear idea of what Hayden had been talking about for months in terms of the Kevin Tremblay lecture.

"I don't know. I haven't figured it out that far yet."

"Well, you should be thinking about it *now*."

Kevin convinced me to come clean to Coach and the team…so that next year, Alice Bell could play for the Falcons. And Alice Bell could have the chance of being scouted by the

United State's national women's team.

"You could make a life playing hockey, Alice. Isn't that what you want?" Kevin had said.

Of course it was. I just never thought Alice had a future in hockey.

I take a big bite of my burger and look around. Tomorrow, I'll tell Coach the truth and Alice will take her first step to being a professional hockey player.

But for today, I'll just enjoy this moment. Whatever happens, we'll make our own happiness. Together.

"Picture time!" Eleanor trills. "Squeeze together!"

I push against Hayden, and Madison wraps an arm around me. Xander muscles in beside us. A genuine smile takes over my face. When I look back at this picture, what will I see?

Madison, my best friend. Like a goalie, she's always there, bailing me out of my own messes and giving me backup. Her unfailing support and strength have kept me afloat all season.

Xander, my brother. Like the left wing to my right, he reads my mind like a playbook. I know he would dive into the deep end for me...and always will.

And Hayden. The center of my life. A pillar of confidence, supporting me until I have the strength to make the play on my own. He changes the ice as soon as he steps on it.

When I look at this picture, I will see the team that makes up Alice Bell.

And that is a lineup worth playing for.

Acknowledgments

This story began back when we were tweens playing NHL 2005 on our well-loved PlayStation 2. Of course, the best part of the game was not actually playing hockey, but the create-a-player mode. That's when the first version of the Falcons' roster—and the beginnings of this story—developed: the hot-headed star player, his too-perfect older brother, and of course, the girl in disguise. It took an all-star behind-the-scenes lineup (and a lot of Korean dramas) to turn this idea into Alice and Hayden's story.

A massive thank you to Brenda, editor extraordinaire, for her consistent words of encouragement, belief in our little book, and her ability to bring out the absolute best in a story. Thank you for bringing out the good in Alice!

Thank you to the entire Entangled team! We love you guys so much! To Stacy, Crystal, Riki, Holly, the Crush family, and everyone else involved — we are so grateful for your passion.

To Awnna, for without her enthusiasm, we would never have written this book. Thank you for breaking us out of our writing rut and giving us a reason to pick up our laptops again.

Thank you to our wonderful friends who keep us from being hermits with only make-believe people to talk about. A special thanks to Graeme for weathering the highest highs, the lowest lows, and all that comes between during this wonderful life we share.

And of course, a huge thank you to Mom and Dad. Dad, thank you for raising us on hockey, for answering every hockey question known to man, and for reading to us every night. Mom, thank you for suffering through every game, for patiently waiting as we stalked players in the hotel lobby, and for being our first and most enthusiastic reader. We will treasure our Blackhawks memories, always.

About the Author

Leah and Kate Rooper are sisters from Victoria, British Columbia, Canada. Growing up beside the Pacific Ocean and inside a temperate rainforest fed their sense of adventure as children, and nourished a curiosity for strange and distant lands. They fed this curiosity with books—lots and lots of books. After experiencing the magic of Middle-earth, they began creating their own worlds. When they're not writing, Leah and Kate spend their time blogging and vlogging about their travel adventures and their writing journey. You can visit them at: www.leahkatewrite.com

Also by Leah and Kate Rooper...

JANE UNWRAPPED

Discover more of Entangled Teen Crush's books...

APPROXIMATELY YOURS
a *North Pole, Minnesota* novel by Julie Hammerle

Danny Garland asked out Holly's cousin. Elda is a mess at flirting and has no idea he's Holly's long-time crush, so when she begs Holly to intervene, she does. Holly helps her flirt with him over text. And then again. Now she's stuck texting him as her cousin, and Elda is the one going on the date. Holly thought she could settle for just conversation, but talking with Danny is some kind of magic. He's got the perfect comebacks, she makes him laugh, they text until everyone else is asleep. She just can't ever tell him it's her he's really texting.

BREAKING THE RULES OF REVENGE
an *Endless Summer* novel by Samantha Bohrman

Mallory is tired of being the girl who stays home and practices French horn while her identical twin, Blake, is crowned homecoming queen. So when she has the opportunity to pretend to *be* Blake, she takes it. At camp, she'll spread her wings and emerge a butterfly. Or at least someone who gets kissed by a cute guy. That is, until bad boy Ben shows up, ready to get revenge on Blake—aka Mallory.

Made in the USA
Las Vegas, NV
20 December 2023